If ever in your life you are faced with a choice, a difficult decision, a quandary,

Ask yourself,
"What would Edgar and Ellen do?"

And do exactly the contrary.

Edgar & Ellen

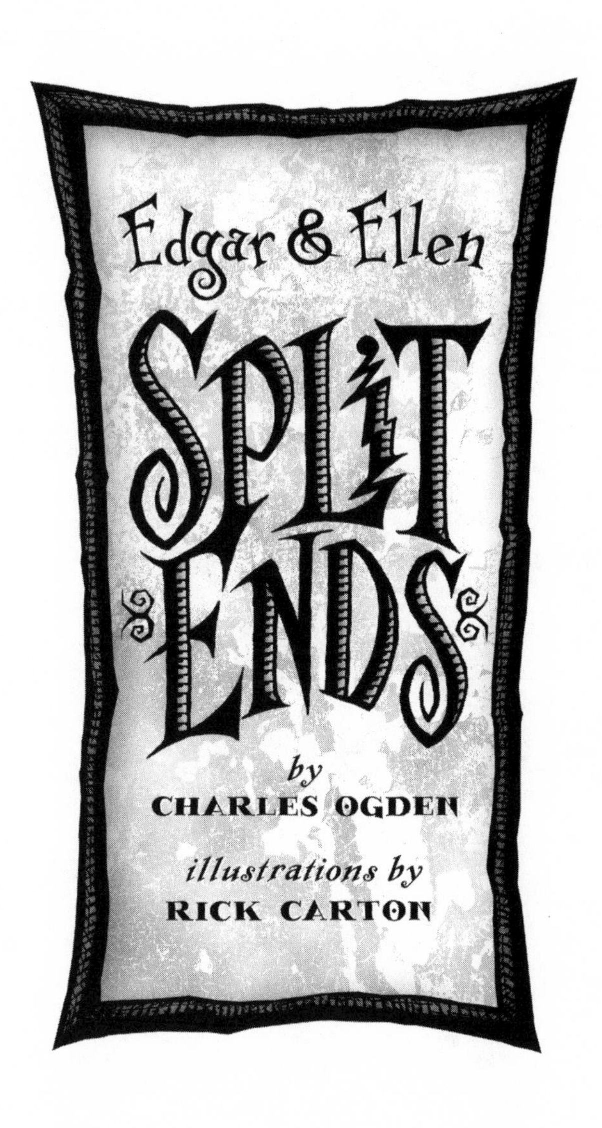

ALADDIN
New York London Toronto Sydney

Watch out for Edgar & Ellen in:

Rare Beasts
Tourist Trap
Under Town
Pet's Revenge
High Wire
Nod's Limbs
Edgar & Ellen Mischief Manual
Hair 'Em Scare 'Em
Hot Air
Frost Bites

ALADDIN
An imprint of Simon & Schuster Children's Publishing Division
1230 Avenue of the Americas, New York, NY 10020

Designed by Star Farm Productions, LLC
The text of this book was set in Bembo.
The illustrations in this book were rendered in pen and ink and digitally enhanced in Photoshop.
Manufactured in the United States of America
First Aladdin edition January 2009
10 9 8 7 6 5 4 3 2 1
Library of Congress Cataloging-in-Publication Data
Ogden, Charles.
Split ends / by Charles Ogden ; illustrated by Rick Carton.—1st Aladdin ed.
p. cm.—(Edgar & Ellen nodyssey ; #3)
Summary: Still in pursuit of the circus fugitives, mischievous twins Edgar and Ellen take separate paths as Ellen visits the unfriendly town of Lach Lufless and Edgar enters the forest home of Squatch the monster.
ISBN-13: 978-1-4169-5466-8
ISBN-10: 1-4169-5466-X
[1. Monsters—Fiction. 2. Twins—Fiction. 3. Brothers and sisters—Fiction. 4. Humorous stories.] I. Carton, Rick, ill. II. Title.
PZ7.O333Sp 2009
[Fic]—dc22
2008045381

Here is my dedication—

To Ellen, for loving as much as I do
The madness and mayhem
and mischief of two.

—Charles

WHERE BACKWOODS AND WATERS MEET...

Prologue

Two figures wearing striped pajamas tumbled headlong into a steaming, smoldering pit of red lava at the bottom of a volcano. Fright and agony were etched across their faces, but nothing—*nothing*—could save them now. It was the end of those terrible twins, Edgar and Ellen.

Stephanie Knightleigh sighed her disappointment at the lopsided drawing in her notebook. It was mere fantasy. In reality the twins had escaped the Black Diamond volcano, each in one piece.

Stephanie flipped through her notebook to pages

filled with scribblings, scientific formulas, and other sketches of doomed stick figures. She sat at the counter of the Bandy Station Café, sipping a cranberry phosphate that was far too weak for her liking. Out the window to her left, freight trains moved through the stockyard, and the station hands scurried to and fro, loading cargo. Stephanie tapped her fingers impatiently, then perused more pages, checking off various things and making new notes. She paused on a dense grid of numbers.

"They're all a little different, but the same," she mumbled. "There has to be a sequence that magnifies the power. But things in the woods seem to be going well, according to him." She sneered. "Won't he be surprised."

"Everything to your liking, miss?" The waitress pointed at Stephanie's glass.

"Hardly," Stephanie snapped. "The porter said he'd have my things ready half an hour ago. I'm going to miss my train. Moss grows faster than you people move." She pushed her glass away. "And this phosphate isn't tart enough."

"I'd say you're tart enough as is, dearie." The waitress snatched up Stephanie's glass and disappeared into the kitchen.

Stephanie huffed and flipped to a page that had a simple list on it:

~~NL~~
~~BD~~
LL
CF
ZZ?
~~QT~~

"Halfway there," she said, and glanced at her watch for the umpteenth time. "What is taking that porter so long?"

Finally a chap in striped overalls entered the café and doffed his cap to Stephanie.

"Miss Knightleigh? She's all packed and ready."

"It's about time," said Stephanie. "Show me."

The porter led Stephanie out through the stockyard, weaving through the rumbling freight trains. They arrived at the very farthest, and the man helped Stephanie into one of the cars. She walked over to a very large crate and inspected it closely, ensuring all the nails and bolts were secure. She plucked a tuft of white hair from an airhole in one of the boards.

"What you got in there anyway?" the porter asked. "Sure was heavy. And I think something inside growled at me when we were getting it in here."

"You must be mistaken," Stephanie said coolly. "This is nothing more than a new type of wool . . . heavier than the common variety."

"Good for winter sweaters, I bet," said the porter. He pulled out a clipboard and looked it over. "You're all set. Your package will be delivered to a . . . Smelterburg? Is that right?"

"That is correct," said Stephanie, and she hopped out of the train car. "And now I must be off to *my* next destination," she added as she left the station.

1. A Game of Dice

"That's Pakatchaloosa money," snorted the captain of the *Sea Witch*. "That rot is worthless in New Pakatchaloosa."

Edgar groaned and put the coins back in his satchel. As he rummaged about for another form of payment, he muttered to himself about exchange rates and gold standards and his general bafflement at the workings of the world's currency. He had won a hefty handful of coins in a game of cards with some dodgy-looking crewmen, and while his winnings had bought him passage on the *Sea Witch,* there wasn't enough left over to cover the candy bar he had been caught "borrowing" from the captain's lunch box. None of Edgar's usual schemes to side-step trouble had seemed to work on the savvy crew of the ferry, and now he was cornered.

"Okay, it looks like I don't have any New Pakatcha-whatever money," said Edgar. "Would you accept a barter for your candy bar? A genuine shark-tooth back scratcher, maybe? Nickel-plated pipe fitting? Mostly uncracked Erlenmeyer flask? Homemade sheriff's badge?"

"Homemade sheriff's badge?" asked the captain, scratching at his eye patch. "What the devil would I do with that?"

"Stop traffic, make arrests, bypass security, con-duct investigations, question suspects—"

"Enough! Eh, I'll take it," said the captain. He snatched the badge. "Now get off my ship and into Grayweather country."

"Grayweather? I thought this was New Palooka," said Edgar.

"When you're a-standing on my boat, you're in New Pakatchaloosa territory," said the captain, pointing to the purple-and-yellow flag flying from an aft flagpole. "Down at the end of the gangplank is Grayweather Province."

"You're sure this is where those circus performers got off?" asked Edgar.

"Oh, aye," said the captain. "I always keep an eye on circus folk. Especially ones as chipper as that lot. Shifty, they were. Kept my one good eye on 'em till they were off my boat. Don't know where they went after that, and don't care to. 'Tweren't but two days ago, so if you intend to settle a score with them, you best get a move on."

The captain practically shoved Edgar down the gangway.

"Okay, okay, I'm going," said Edgar. "Cripes, I thought that badge meant we were square."

"Even when I get the mustard stains off my steering wheel, the bilge water out of the diesel tanks, and every last pair of boxers untied from the flagpole, we *still* won't be square, you imp," growled the captain. "Take your high-seas mischief and be gone."

Edgar walked down the gangway and took in his surroundings. Grayweather Province was mountainous country: The land beyond the harbor spread out in densely forested foothills and peaks and looked uninhabited. Without further guidance it would be nearly impossible to know which way the Midway Irregulars had gone.

"But I know those circus freaks came this way, and I'm going to catch them," said Edgar. Since parting ways with his sister almost three weeks ago, he had taken to talking to himself. ("I know who'll appreciate hearing my brilliant insights," he had said. "Me!") The reindeer he had ridden out of the Arctic wasteland hadn't seemed to mind his prattling—though one night Edgar's snores grew so loud they spooked the beast, and it ran off. Edgar had had to follow the trail of the Midway Irregulars on foot, which had been fairly easy until he reached the coast. Fortunately, he had come to a harbor where he met the captain of the *Sea Witch*, who confirmed ferrying the circus kids over to Grayweather.

Now on the far side, Edgar thought to seek out more information on the Midway Irregulars and where they might have gone.

Walking along the harbor, Edgar came upon a group of dockhands playing a game of dice. Edgar felt in his satchel for his own pair of dice, which looked normal to the naked eye but really were fitted with remote-controlled gyroscopes of Edgar's own design.

"Hey, fellas, mind if I rest my feet for a bit and join you?"

The dockhands looked up at the scrawny boy in striped footie pajamas, then at one another. Smiles broke out across their sooty faces.

"Why, sure there, lad," said one, who was missing most of his teeth. "Pull up a stool right next to me, here. You ever play dice before?"

"No. Never," said Edgar innocently.

"Even better," said Toothless. The guy next to him, who had a black eye, elbowed him in the ribs.

"What my friend means is, we'll be happy to explain the rules," said Black Eye.

"That's mighty nice of you," said Edgar, and he settled in.

"Sevens and elevens easy up, no loosey deucies, boxcars on top," said Black Eye, rolling the dice.

"You all haven't seen a gaggle of ragtag kids come through here, have you?" Edgar asked as the dice were passed around.

"Yeah, yeah, the *Sea Witch* ferried a crew of nutters like that across the channel a couple days ago," Toothless said. "All smiles and juggling and carrying on, the five of them. What you want them for?"

"They're traveling the world stealing a rare substance that can make a person live forever," Edgar said. "We're not sure what they're doing with it. I suspect they're mixing samples from different locations to make something terrible."

Edgar palmed the dice when they reached him and secretly replaced them with his own gyroscopic dice. He rolled a pair of sixes. "Is that good?"

"Beginner's luck," growled a dockhand whose entire neck was covered in tattoos. Each man handed Edgar a coin.

"Sounds like a pack of right rotten souls you're after, eh?" said Black Eye.

"Not usually," said Edgar. "But at the moment, the Midway Irregulars are under the influence of a hypnotic potion made from the tears of a near-mythical beast."

"You don't say," said Toothless. "Bah," he added as his dice turned up snake eyes.

"I'm carrying some unique seeds that are the antidote to their hypnosis," said Edgar. "The fate of humanity hinges on me catching up to them. Er, so I'm told by my two-hundred-year-old mad-scientist friend."

"Boy, I have heard some whoppers in my day,

but this takes all. You hit your head when the ferry docked?" asked Black Eye.

"No, just an overactive imagination, I guess," said Edgar, rolling an eleven. The men all groaned and handed over more coins. "You wouldn't happen to know which way they went, would you?"

Toothless gestured toward shore, where a path wound up into a pine-lined mountain pass. "They went thataway."

"What's up there?" asked Edgar.

The dockhands eyed one another warily.

"Trees," said Black Eye. "Miles and miles of 'em. And wild creatures none too friendly to humans. No one goes into Footwood Forest without a guide. If your circus friends went up there by themselves, likely as not they're dead already."

The men shuddered. Edgar pretended not to notice and picked up the dice, rolling a seven.

"Well, it must just be my lucky day." He chuckled, gathering up everyone's coins. But as he did, Tattoo grabbed his wrist, and the remote button used to control the dice fell out of his sleeve.

"I knew it! Cheat!" shouted Tattoo as the other dockhands jumped to their feet. Edgar backed away from them toward the shore.

"Gee, fellas, it sure has been . . . educational. Great game!" He started to run as Tattoo lunged at him, seizing him by the collar. Edgar threw all his purloined coins onto the dock and, in the men's haste to retrieve them, managed to struggle free. He bolted for the forest, zigzagging up the steep path until he had disappeared amid the bracken.

Back on the docks, the men had gathered up their money and stood looking after the fleeing boy. None moved to follow him.

"He'll get his," said Black Eye. "He'll be lost before dusk, and that's when the Squatch will get 'im."

2. Follow the White Hair

Ellen shielded her eyes from the light of the rising sun. She could see that overnight the landscape had gone from scrubby brushland to a lush green expanse dotted with ponds and bogs. The glare off the ponds made Ellen squint, and Pet clamped its single eyeball shut.

"Beauty is really annoying," groused Ellen.

It wasn't long before Ellen missed that annoyance:

The rising sun was soon obscured by a permanent blanket of gray clouds. As the morning wore on, a weak rain fell every few hours, wetting Ellen and Pet just enough to make them uncomfortable.

Their reindeer, Hjort (Ellen had named it for an unfortunate sound the beast made after eating too much lichen), clomped slowly along the muddy road. Ellen slouched across its neck, too weary to sit up straight. She'd lost count of how many days they'd been traveling, but she thought it was close to three weeks. At first Hjort had kept a brisk pace, and they had covered many miles. But after a week, the exhausted reindeer could only plod along, and they had to stop frequently to scavenge for food in the cold and the damp. Ellen's joints were stiff and achy, and with nothing to eat but berries and bark and the occasional grub, she could barely keep from tumbling off Hjort's back.

Pet sat atop the reindeer's head, its eye peeled for the white hairs that were their bread crumbs. Every now and then, Pet would see one caught in a bush or branch, and Ellen would know they were still on the right track. The hair belonged to Yehti, the large white relative of Pet's that Stephanie Knightleigh had petnapped.

Ellen, tired, hungry, and with no clue where in the world they were, was beginning to lose hope that they'd ever catch Stephanie. More than anything she wanted to confer with her brother. But Edgar was somewhere in the opposite direction, chasing a different chapter of their adventure.

Sure, she had Pet, who was comforting company—Edgar was completely on his own—but Ellen had never realized how much she missed hearing another human voice. To fill the silence, she talked at length to Pet, who of course could make no verbal reply. Such one-sided conversation was not particularly satisfying, nor were the songs she sang to herself, for she had no brother there to sing along with her:

From frozen field to swampy shire,
Wits left to linger in the mire,
Journey on, though clues expire,
Journey on, and never tire.
The ice has melted into lakes,
Though not that it a difference makes.
My back, my rear, my belly aches—
Some action *please, for goodness' sakes!*
And, Brother, say, how do you fare
Out in the great wide world somewhere?

At this point, neither she nor Pet had seen a strand of white hair in days, and Ellen was afraid they'd lost Stephanie's trail altogether. Ellen usually would discuss problems like this with Edgar, and together they would reach a solution. Even their bickering kept her on her toes. Now, Ellen was fairly sure she'd lost her edge entirely, maybe back at that river they'd had to ford.

The rain started again, and Hjort's hooves splashed in the muddy puddles. Pet saw that they were approaching a signpost and, beyond that, a three-pronged fork in the road. With a tendril Pet pulled one of Ellen's pigtails, rousing her.

"What is it?" she asked dully. Pet pointed at the signpost.

BAIRN ← 5
PERTHLY → 8
LACH LUFLESS ↑ 10.5

The arrow for Bairn pointed to the left, the one for Perthly pointed right, and for Lach Lufless, straight ahead.

"Lach Lufless?" Ellen gasped "Pet! We've done it!"

Pet scratched its eyelid in bewilderment.

"Remember the Black Diamond Glacier, Pet? Those letters we saw scribbled in Stephanie's hotel room?"

Pet nodded at once and leaped to the ground, where it traced letters in the mud: *NL + BD + LL + CF.*

"Exactly," said Ellen. "*NL* for Nod's Limbs, *BD* for Black Diamond . . ."

Pet waved its tendrils, cheerleader-like, in the shape of a pair of *L*s.

Ellen smiled for the first time in days, and Pet bounced merrily up onto Hjort's head. "Onward to Lach Lufless, Hjort. Stephanie'll be in our grasp by lunchtime!"

3. A Gripping Sight

They traveled the road for an hour. The winding path rose somewhat, and the terrain became punctuated by sharp rocks that stuck out of the ground like knives. The countryside of ponds continued to sprawl around them, and as they climbed the road, they could see that each pool drained into the next in a series of rivulets and little waterfalls. At one point the road turned to crumbling cobblestone, and Ellen spotted low stone walls racing across the green fields, and the occasional stone hut dotted the landscape. But at no point did they see any people or signs of a town.

The rain had stopped, but the air was cool, and Ellen pulled her damp parka tighter around her. Over the crest of a hillock, she glimpsed something glittering in the distance. As they topped the hill, she saw that it wasn't just another pond; a vast lake spread out before her. The farthest edges disappeared in a faint shroud of mist, making an accurate guess of its size impossible.

Along its southern coast, she could make out buildings and the spire of a clock tower reaching into the sky.

"I never thought I'd be so relieved to see signs of civilization," she said. "Even if it *is* another zombie copy of Nod's Limbs, I'll take it."

Pet nodded its eyeball.

The lake reflected the gray sky, and even the green of the rolling moors looked as pale and dull as stone. It was a lonely place, this corner of the world she'd stumbled upon, somehow even lonelier

than remote and icy Frøsthaven. Even in that frozen wilderness, she and Edgar had quickly come upon friendly locals, who had turned their bleak conditions into fun and frolic. Not just frolic, in fact, but insanely cheery goofiness of such magnitude it resembled their own hometown. Nod's Limbs and Frøsthaven—both homes to a mysterious balm spring—were equally batty for public festivals, civic self-esteem, and irrepressible good cheer.

Here, though, there were no such signs of giddiness to signify a balm spring close by. And Ellen was fairly certain Stephanie wouldn't have traveled here just for the water-skiing. Could *LL* stand for something else?

"Maybe we just have to get closer, then we'll start getting the glee club routine," Ellen said to Pet.

Squawk!

The screech made Ellen jump and nearly topple off Hjort's back. It was the first noise she'd heard besides the whispering wind or her own voice in many hours, and she looked around for its source.

A dead and leafless tree, its bark white with age, stood a little ways off, and on one of its branches perched a large raven. It stared at the travelers, then *squawked* again.

"Hello, friend, what do you want?" said Ellen, then caught herself. "Cripes, I am going batty, talking to a raven like it's going to answer me."

But to her surprise, the raven flew down from the branch and glided toward her. Now, for the first time, she saw that it clutched something white in a gnarled talon. As it flew over her, just barely missing her head, it dropped the object into her lap, then returned to its post on the dead tree.

Ellen examined the projectile: a rolled piece of paper tied with twine. She eyed the raven curiously. Something about it seemed familiar, but she couldn't place it. The last thing she was expecting in this far-flung land was a missive from a bird.

She slipped off the twine and unfolded the paper. A gasp escaped her lips as she read the short note scrawled in a too-familiar hand:

My dear twins! Old Grip has been patrolling the skies, and unless his frantic dance was a peculiar new tic, then he has indeed spotted your telltale stripes this morning. How lovely to know your tracking skills have served you well. Follow Grip to our hidden abode. We have much to discuss, not least our latest findings concerning

Ronan and the rest of the circus. Hurry, my friends, Dahlia has been boiling a batch of rams' bladders all morning. Scrumptious!

Yours, Augie

"Nod!" Ellen cried, and Pet jumped onto her shoulder and hugged her neck. "Of course—that's Grip, one of Nod's homing ravens. I knew I recognized him, I just couldn't imagine, here, of all places . . ." She trailed off as the raven screeched again and left its perch. It flew down the road toward the lake, stopped on a hedge, and looked back at them expectantly.

"Yes, yes, we're coming!" Ellen called, and she drove Hjort forward after the raven, which flew ahead of them, stopping whenever it had gone too far.

Ellen couldn't believe her luck, that she and Pet should have trailed Stephanie to the exact place Augustus Nod had come. Nod, the old man kept alive for two centuries by balm from a spring underneath the twins' old house, had left at the same time as the twins, also in search of Stephanie.

"If he's found Heimertz, then things are really

looking up," said Ellen. The twins' smiley groundskeeper had disappeared along with the rest of his circus family. His wife, Madame Dahlia, plant tamer and something of a mentor to Ellen, had gone with Nod in search of her husband. "I can't wait to see them, Pet, and find out what's going on. Hopefully they'll have more answers than we do."

The road followed the lake's edge toward Lach Lufless, but soon Grip veered off it, swerving into the low-lying brush inland. There was no path to speak of, just scratchy brambles and heath, and Hjort had trouble finding footing. Finally Ellen and Pet were forced to dismount. Ellen patted the reindeer affectionately on its flank.

"Thanks, Hjort. You're dismissed. Now scamper off and, you know, start a reindeer family or something."

Hjort didn't scamper, but it did flop down in a rather relieved way and nibble some lichen off a rock.

"Uh-oh, we better scram, Pet," said Ellen, "before he starts *hjort*ing again."

4. A Toast to Good Health

Ellen and Pet followed Grip deeper into the brush to a stand of twisted birch trees. Ellen's heart leaped.

"I can't wait to see them!" she bubbled. When Pet gave her a surprised look, Ellen coughed and scowled. "Er, because I'm hungry. I could use a hot meal, that's all. I don't *miss* anyone, Pet, obviously."

Something glinted through the sparse trees, and Ellen recognized the gunmetal gray material that made up Nod's dirigible. Only it was not just now in its dirigible form. Augustus Nod, mad genius, could never take the simplest route to solve a problem: thus, many of the objects he invented served more than one purpose. His dirigible was one such success; when grounded, it could fold out into a massive tent, which provided ample shelter from all forms of weather. Nod and Madame Dahlia had made camp in a clearing amid the birch trees.

As Ellen and Pet neared the tent, the flap lifted, and Nod emerged. His crazy white hair blew in the breeze, and his skin looked a bit more weathered than Ellen remembered; the exertion of travel and hunting their missing friends had not agreed with him.

"Ellen!" he exclaimed, holding open his arms.

"You're radiant! What a delight to see you!"

"Radiant?" Ellen asked. "You've either lost your eyesight or your mind."

"Neither, my dear—I'm just so happy to see you again."

"Wow, you must be feeling good," said Ellen. "From the look of you, I thought maybe you weren't doing so well . . ."

"Pish-posh," said Nod. "It's this northern air, my dear. It's done wonders for my health—I feel like a schoolboy, I tell you!"

"Well, don't worry, you still look really, really old."

"Ha ha! Good one, Ellen!" Nod put one arm around Ellen's shoulders, and tousled Pet's mane. Then he looked around. "Ah, has Edgar fallen behind you? Is he sneaking up as part of another ill-advised prank?" Nod gasped. "Tell me he isn't . . . oh, perish the thought—"

"He's fine," said Ellen. "We split up to track our enemies better. You'll never believe who—"

"Oh, dear." Nod's face clouded. "I never expected this. I was counting on *both* of you being here. It's essential that we gather everyone *at once*. Confound your unpredictable impulses!"

Anger welled up in Nod's voice. Ellen was used to such bad-tempered outbursts and felt great relief that Nod's haggard body was still brimming with spirit. But his dark expression passed as soon as it had arrived.

"Well, we shall cope," he said cheerily. "We have an important mission to complete, and you play a major part, Ellen. And by important mission, I mean . . . *lunch!*" Nod threw open the tent flap to reveal Madame Dahlia stirring a thick stew over an open fire. "Dahlia! One of our adventurers has returned, and she is famished."

The smell emanating from the tent could scarcely have been defined as "scrumptious," as Nod's note had proclaimed. Still, with Ellen's stomach rumbling, the scent of ram-bladder stew made her knees wobble and her mouth drool. That, combined with the sight of her old friend Madame Dahlia ladling out a bowlful, made Ellen practically squeal with glee. She resisted and instead threw her arms around the sizable Dahlia, who hugged her back.

"Ellen! We have waited, and finally you come!"

"You were waiting for me? How did you know I was coming here?"

Madame Dahlia glanced at Nod.

"Because the clues lead here, of course," Madame Dahlia replied. "Augustus was certain Miss Stephanie would be leaving a trail for the following."

"And I knew you twins would be on her like dimples on a pickle," said Nod. He picked up Pet and scratched the creature behind its eyelid. Pet closed its eye in rapture.

"Have you seen her?" Ellen's eyes lit up. "Did you stop her?"

"Plenty of time to talk about her." Nod guided Ellen to a table made from gathered logs. "Let's get your strength back."

"I have so much to tell you," said Ellen, sitting down, "and so many questions. Do you know what Stephanie's plans are? Where is she now? Is there a balm spring here? What do you know of Heimertz?"

"In time, in time," said Madame Dahlia. She plunked the bowl of odorous stew in front of Ellen and stirred it with a spoon. "Fresh *haggum*, a local stew. Will warm and nourish you."

Ellen bypassed the spoon and poured the *haggum* directly into her mouth with a gluttonous *hjort*ing sound.

Madame Dahlia poured Ellen a glass of a dark red juice.

"Your poor parched throat," she said. "Soothing drink is made from locally harvested berries."

Ellen pushed the glass away.

"No thanks, Dahlia. I've feasted on enough of those berries to last a lifetime."

Nod and Madame Dahlia exchanged furtive looks, but Ellen was too engrossed in her soup to notice. Nor did she notice that Nod had stopped scratching Pet and had slipped the creature inside a blanket-lined picnic basket. Pet opened its eye in alarm just as Nod flipped the lid over the top and secured it with an iron padlock.

He pushed the glass back toward Ellen.

"I really think you'll like it, Ellen. It has many healthful benefits. Helps blemishes and ingrown toenails."

"Since when have you been concerned about health?" Ellen pushed the glass away again.

"This isn't about health." Nod pushed the glass back. "It's about the success of our mission."

"Look, mission accomplished. I ate the food. I just don't want the drink. What is your problem?"

"Augustus, you should not be forcing Ellen to try something she is not wanting," said Madame Dahlia. "There are other ways to make her drink."

"That's right—what?" Ellen demanded, but at that moment Madame Dahlia seized her from behind. The large woman held Ellen firmly and pulled down on her pigtails so Ellen's face turned upward. Nod approached with the glass of red juice, and for the first time, Ellen noticed a deadness in his eyes.

"Oh no, Stephanie got to you!" Ellen struggled in Madame Dahlia's grasp, but the woman was far too powerful. "She hypnotized you with Pet tears, didn't she?"

"Stephanie gives us instructions, yes," said Madame Dahlia. "We are feeling it is necessary to follow them."

"Soon you will see. You will be as happy following her as we are." Nod shoved the rim of the glass to Ellen's lips and tilted it up. Juice spilled down her chin, but her lips didn't part. Depending on how strongly Nod had laced the drink with the tears, a single drop of it could turn Ellen into a Stephanie-loving lemming.

Ellen thrashed her head and spat the juice off her lips. "Pet!" she cried. "Attack!"

"My one-eyed comrade can do no such thing," said Nod. "He has been packed away—comfortably, I hope, old friend?"

Nod looked over at the picnic basket, and Ellen could see strands of Pet's hair surging through the wicker like an explosion of dental floss. Some of its tendrils had even wrapped around the padlock as if trying to smother it, but the lock held firm.

"Not so comfortably, I'm afraid, but the result is the same. Your situation is quite hopeless, my dear," said Nod. "I'm afraid we must try a new tactic."

He pulled an oily funnel from a toolbox—a crusty old thing with years' worth of blackened motor oil congealed on its sides.

"Here we are," said Nod. "Perhaps this device will put an end to all this unpleasant struggling."

He placed the narrow end of the funnel against Ellen's lips. She knew it would only be a matter of moments before she was chugging zombie juice.

"W-wait!" she sputtered. "I'll do it!" Nod relented slightly, and Ellen said quickly, "I'll drink it. Willingly. I'll join you. With a big, fat smile on my face!"

"With a smile? Why, that's all I'm asking for," Nod said, pulling the funnel away. "No need for this beastly funnel business. No tricks, though . . ."

"Of course not," said Ellen. "After all, it's clear

you've thought of everything—even using a genuine Stock Maiden 900 to lock that basket."

"Eh?" said Nod.

"Yes, sir, a *Stock Maiden 900.* Brilliant!" Ellen said loudly. Though Edgar was the master locksmith of the twins, Ellen had escaped her fair share of traps and easily recognized one of the most complex devices in her brother's arsenal. And while she had no clue how to unlock it, she knew someone who did. "You yourself know, Nod, a Stock Maiden 900 is one of the most notoriously difficult locks to break."

Nod and Madame Dahlia looked at Ellen curiously, as if she were speaking a foreign tongue. To Ellen's relief, they did not notice the braid of hair that was busy with the lock behind them.

"Yesiree," Ellen continued with a smile. "I only know two people in the whole world who can pick a lock like that. One of them is Edgar. And the other one . . . isn't even a person."

Nod's eyes widened and he snapped his head toward the picnic basket. The Stock Maiden 900 lay on the ground and the basket's lid was wide open.

"Oh, fiddlesticks," he said.

Like a small, fuzzy ninja, Pet leaped from seemingly nowhere onto Madame Dahlia's head and jabbed its tendrils into her eyes. She howled, and her hands flew to her face, letting go of Ellen's hair.

Ellen lunged forward and pushed Nod as hard as she could. The old man stumbled backward over the picnic basket and crashed to the ground. He dropped the glass, and it shattered.

"Sorry!" Ellen called as she ran to the tent flap. "Let's try this again when you're not brainwashed!"

Pet jumped from Madame Dahlia's fallen form into Ellen's arms, and together they fled the tent and scrambled away.

5. The Shrub Speaks

"Blisters between my toes . . . nothing to eat but pine needles . . . no one to talk to in this endless, empty wood," Edgar groused to himself as he made his way up the mountain. "I almost miss that candy-coated hometown of mine." He shook himself. "What am I *saying*?"

As he crested the pass between the mountains, Edgar stopped for a breather. A canopy of red and yellow leaves hung above, and those that had fallen to the ground spread out before him like a flame-colored blanket. And right at his feet, in a mound of moose droppings, he saw the unmistakable imprint of a cowboy boot.

"Aha! Careless Gonzalo!" said Edgar. "If he keeps leaving me clues like this, I'll be on him before he can say *dunk tank*."

"What makes you so sure?" Edgar asked himself.

"Well, have I ever let you down?" Edgar replied.

"No. Not once, you clever devil," he said, and he gave himself a pat on the back. He reached into his satchel for an old pencil case and poured its contents into his palm: five bone-white *Nepenthes arcticus* seeds. The little pods seemed harmless, but Edgar knew better—they were the only cure for the Irregulars' hypnosis. Five seeds, one for each Midway Irregular.

"Simple," said Edgar. "Catch up to them, get the seeds down their throats, then . . ." He paused.

"Then what?" he asked himself.

"Let's jump off that bridge when we get to it," he responded.

He poured the seeds back into the pencil case, hoisted his satchel, and set off along the path.

Now, as anyone who has done a bit of hiking knows, not every path through the woods can be trusted. Some paths will lead a traveler smartly and swiftly to his destination, but others have a taste for trickery. Such paths may start off with the promise of a safe, well-traveled route, but after a bit of wandering thither and yon, they play catch-me-if-you-can through unexpected thickets and patches of snareweed. These paths find it funny to lead wanderers far astray of their course, and they succeed at an alarmingly high rate.

Thus did Edgar meander from one path to another, until he was hopelessly lost in the dense forest. It had been hours since he'd seen any trace of the Midway Irregulars, and the cloud-filled sky obscured both the sun and Edgar's sense of direction.

His feet were sore, his arms ached from carrying his satchel, and the only food he'd been able to find were spiky, foul-tasting berries. And now the sun was setting, the sky growing darker every minute. Edgar tried to sing a song to keep his spirits up:

It's not too cold—my skin is tough,
And my stomach's full enough,
Good thing I'm made of sterner stuff
Or these woods might seem grim.
Sure, Ellen would know every plant—
What one can eat, and what one can't—
But I can cope, though food be scant,
And the light grown dim . . .

Edgar flopped down next to a bush, into a pile of fallen leaves. They would have to do for both mattress and blanket. He nestled in, covering himself with leaves up to his head. They were dry, which Edgar was thankful for, but hardly soft, and he spent the night tossing and turning on the hard, cold earth. Sunrise was a blessing, and he rose with the dawn.

His stomach gurgled. Edgar pulled some of the berries from his satchel and winced.

"Guess it's time for another one of you horrid things," he said. He lisped somewhat—his tongue was still sore from the last berry he'd eaten. He closed his eyes and opened his mouth wide.

"Don't eat that," said the bush next to him.

Edgar jumped. He looked closely at the lumpy shrub.

"Fantastic," said Edgar sarcastically. "These things also make me hallucinate."

"No, but nettleberries will turn you purple in places you'd never expect," said the bush. "Look, go suck on a loonroot if you're hungry, then beat it. You're going to ruin everything!"

"Wait—you're not a hallucination; you're a guy in camouflage!" said Edgar. He could see a pair of eyeballs within the foliage. "What the heck are you doing in that getup? Hunting caribou?"

"Something like that," said the bush gruffly. An ugly yellow hunk of something tumbled from the branches. "Here's some loonroot. Now get lost!"

"Have you seen five circus fugitives pass through here?" asked Edgar.

"Circus *what*? Kid, the circus isn't due in Cougar Falls until next year. Now skedaddle! You're going to spook the wildlife."

"Aha! So the circus *does* come around here!" exclaimed Edgar. "Cougar Falls, eh? CF . . . CF . . . Yes, I must be getting close."

"Too close—*to me*," said the bush. "Head back to town and let me do my job, eh?"

"Whatever you say, shrubby," said Edgar. "I've got to get back to tracking anyway." He picked up his satchel and stomped off, but not before grabbing the bizarre root.

"Yes, yes, it all fits with Stephanie's clues. This CF must have a balm spring, and that's where I'll find my circus quarry . . ."

As Edgar chewed the loonroot ("Appalling!" he cried between bites. "Nasty!"), he examined every twig and branch for signs of having been broken by passing circus types. For the better part of an hour, he followed a slender set of footprints that might have been left by an acrobat like Mab or Merrick. But eventually the prints disappeared among the fallen leaves, and soon he was lost once more.

At last he sat down in a clearing and tossed aside his gnawed-on loonroot. His stomach still gurgled, and he plucked a juicy-looking flower blossom from a vine. He opened his mouth to take a bite.

"Don't eat that," said a bush. "Those things *will* make you hallucinate."

"*You again?*" cried Edgar. "Are you following me?"

"Following *you*?" The bush laughed. "Kid, you ran yourself in circles. You were following your own footsteps!"

The bush stood up. To Edgar it appeared as if the shrub had spat out a fully-grown lumberjack. The man wore green hunter's coveralls and a plaid shirt, and now that he was standing, Edgar could see the black twine that held branches to the man's limbs. The burly fellow flicked twigs from his black beard.

"It's plain to see I'm not getting any results today," he said. He looked Edgar over. "Well, you sure as heck aren't from Cougar Falls, eh?"

"Of course not," said Edgar. "As you can tell, I'm a sophisticated world traveler. I've seen more wonders than you'd ever believe—"

"All in footie pajamas," said the man, "and no coat. Not what I'd call the uniform of the experienced traveler."

Edgar blinked hard. First the crew of the *Sea*

Witch, then the dockhands, and now this shrub dweller—they all seemed hard to fool. Back in Nod's Limbs, most folks could be tricked with a well-told untruth. They also had a dippy habit of ignoring Edgar and Ellen's bizarre form of dress, along with several other obvious details, such as their usual proximity to disaster and mayhem.

"You—you're no zombie of niceness," said Edgar. "Maybe Cougar Falls isn't the place I'm looking for . . ."

"Zombie of niceness? Haw!" The man guffawed. "That sure describes Cougar Falls. That's why I live out here—I don't exactly fit in."

Edgar nodded. "I can relate."

"I've got to say, Cougar Falls doesn't seem your style," said the man, looking Edgar up and down. "What's your name, kid?"

"I'm . . ." Edgar paused. "Sir Salvatore Shipsailington. Renowned explorer."

"Sir Salvatore? Now *that's* a stretcher if I ever heard one," said the man. "But I like it anyway, Sally. Suits you. My name is Gristly Jefferson. Professional monster hunter. I don't suppose you've seen Ol' Footsie in your travels through the woods, have you?"

6. Trap It Up

"Old *what*?" said Edgar.

"Oh, come on. You've never heard of Ol' Footsie? The Squatch?"

"I think you're the one who ate the flower blossom, pal."

Gristly Jefferson peeled off his bush costume. "Another nonbeliever," he growled. "You'll see. Everyone will see, when I bring back photographic evidence that it exists." Gristly patted a long-lensed camera strapped to his back.

"This Squatch—is it some kind of hairy beast?" asked Edgar anxiously.

"Sure is."

"With one great big eyeball?"

"I don't know about that," said Gristly Jefferson. "It's got two great big feet, though."

"Feet?" Edgar slumped. "Can't be it, then. I've, uh, seen a lot of monsters in my day, and they're all one-eyed hairballs . . . no feet."

"Well, not Ol' Footsie," said Gristly. "Judging by his tracks, he's at least nine feet tall. I met a guy once who told me the Squatch had him in his powerful jaws—almost bit him in half!—but he managed to get away by jamming a pine branch up the beast's nose."

Edgar mulled this over. Based on his and Ellen's finding Yehti in the Arctic, he suspected that each balm spring might have its own Pet-like beast living nearby. But Gristly's description of the creature's two large feet didn't jibe at all. Nevertheless, where there were Pet-like creatures, there were bound to be balm springs.

Edgar cracked his knuckles, deep in thought.

"I've got an idea," he said. "Let me help you hunt Ol' Footsie. I can be useful—just show me where to look. Point me toward the most likely spot to find it and, you know, let me take a shift."

Gristly let out a hearty laugh. "Good gravy, there, Sally. You can barely tell a pinecone from a pin cushion, you think you can track a Squatch?"

"I am more than capable," said Edgar.

Gristly Jefferson contemplated Edgar a moment, then waved him over to a thicket and parted the branches. Within, Edgar could see ropes and pinions and steel cables—a rudimentary net trap. "You see how big this contraption is? This is no mere grizzly bear we're after here, but a true beast, eh? Hey, be careful!"

Edgar had stepped into the middle of the trap. "Bah, this will never do," he said. "Look here, you've got too much tension on the aft cables. If Footsie triggers it from the other direction, this trap won't ever spring."

"Uh . . . really?" said Gristly.

"And if you're going to use a net, you need the support bars to move relative to the frame, not *contrary* to it," continued Edgar. He pulled a hammer and a metal eye bracket from his satchel. "Here, if we run an extra cable thusly, we can relieve some of the pressure on your trigger mechanism, and make the crosswise cables more secure at the same time . . ."

Gristly sat back as Edgar deftly handled the guts of the trap. It was quick work for Edgar, who had ample experience snaring ornery creatures such as sisters and one-eyed hairballs.

When he had finished, he stood back and admired his work. "Better! If we had a titanium brace for the swing arm, we'd be set. But this will do for now."

Gristly Jefferson slapped him on the back again. It hurt.

"Haw! I like you, Sally. You're an odd duck, but you sure know your way around traps." The man

scratched his beard. "If I teach you a few deep-woods survival tactics, maybe . . . well, maybe you won't be so hopeless in the wilderness. And, in exchange, you can perfect my snares."

And just like that, Edgar was in the monster-hunting business.

7. Tread Lightleigh

"Well, that was disturbing," said Ellen. She and Pet had found shelter in a small quarry away from the lake, and it seemed that they had lost Nod and Madame Dahlia. "They're hypnotized, and that can mean only one thing—Stephanie's somewhere around here."

Pet nodded at her and jumped off the rock it sat on.

"You're right, Pet, we should keep moving," said Ellen. "The best thing to do now is head toward town and find some sign of Stephanie."

Off they set, soon stumbling back onto the shoreline road that led to Lach Lufless, Pet riding on Ellen's shoulder. They looked back frequently to make sure no one was following them, but all they ever saw were stones and the gray clouds overhead.

Soon they came to a marina, or, at least, what passed for one in Lach Lufless. Decrepit-looking dinghies and rowboats, many of them listing as if taking on water, were tethered to decaying wooden posts. No people were about, sailing or swimming or participating in any other water activities Ellen assumed most boat-owning types enjoy.

She would have strode past these pitiful docks completely, if Pet hadn't started jumping up and down and pointing to a boat at the far end of a dock.

"Easy, Pet, it's just a . . ." Ellen peered more closely at the craft. ". . . a fancy new speedboat. *That* sticks out a bit."

Pet led Ellen down the dock toward a boat that was, indeed, quite unlike the other ill-constructed vessels bobbing nearby. This was a high-tech speedboat with a gleaming black hull, a set of harpoons strapped to its sides, and a radar array on the roof of its cabin. Across the stern, written in florid letters, was *Tread Lightleigh*.

"This *has* to be Stephanie," said Ellen. "Who else but a Knightleigh would come up with such a dumb name?"

The two snoops leaped nimbly onto the deck of the craft, but there was not much to see there beyond its spotless rails and orderly coils of nylon rope. It was inside the cabin that Ellen wanted to go, and frankly, with the master of the Stock Maiden 900 at her side, access was a foregone conclusion.

The cabin was pitch black, and Ellen immediately bumped her head on the low ceiling.

"Ow!" she said. "Cripes, Edgar may look ridiculous carrying that satchel all the time, but one of his flashlights sure would come in handy right now."

Pet found a free cord and, with a tug, opened the blinds of a tiny window. In the dim light, Ellen could see around the cabin.

It was cramped, with barely enough space for a small table, a couch, and some computer equipment. Even in this tiny space, however, Ellen noticed, someone had made space for a bulky rack full of hair-care supplies and scented soaps.

"Ha!" Ellen exclaimed. "What a giveaway."

Next she examined the table. It was covered with maps and diagrams and sonar readouts, none of which she understood. She accidentally bumped the computer monitor, and it flashed to life. The screen filled with random dots and lines, and it began beeping at her. Ellen pressed various buttons, but the beeping only got louder.

"Pet, help me turn it off. Stupid computer! Hush your ones and zeroes!"

Ellen hammered away on random keys, but Pet calmly yanked the cord out of the wall. The beeping stopped, and the screen faded to black.

"Edgar would know what all of this means," said Ellen. "Tiresome diagrams and printouts are just his cup of poison."

The only other items of interest she found were a wetsuit and some gleaming scuba equipment. Before she could explore further, Pet jumped back onto her shoulder and swiveled her head toward the cabin entrance.

Someone was outside. They heard heavy footsteps—too heavy to be Stephanie's—walk up the dock and then felt the boat rock as someone leaped aboard. Ellen and Pet kept very still, scarcely daring to breathe. As the footfalls clomped back and forth on the deck above, Ellen backed into the closet, contorting her body to fit in among the scuba gear. She silently closed the door.

Not a moment too soon. They heard the cabin door open and the footsteps climb down the stairs.

All was quiet for a moment as, Ellen guessed, the intruder was looking around, hopefully deciding that everything was as it should be.

And then the door to the closet swung open and a beam of light hit Ellen's eyes, blinding her.

"Law breakers!" said a voice behind the light. "Caught in the act!"

8. LL Law

"Oh, you've done it now," said the voice, and a hand grabbed Ellen's shoulder. It pulled her from the closet and into the cabin. It was only then that Ellen got a good look at her opponent.

It was a policeman, or that's what Ellen suspected. He wore a dark blue tunic and a rounded bobby's hat such as an officer of the law would wear, but his pants and unlaced boots were as muddy as a gardener's. He carried a nightstick, from which protruded a wicked-looking hook.

"Unpleasantly loud beeping," he said gruffly. "I could hear it from the shore. That's the sort of activity that causes disquiet, girlie. And Lach Lufless doesn't tolerate disquiet. Why, hang on . . ." He scrunched up his face and scrutinized her from head to foot. "You're not the same girlie I've seen mucking about on this craft. Who are you, and what were you doing here?"

Ellen eyed him for a moment. Though Edgar lauded her as a master of deception, she preferred the term *truth enhancer.* It was all about what kind of story to tell a particular person—what was this fellow here, for example, willing to believe? She decided to go with blunt simplicity.

"What did it look like I was doing? I was cleaning out the closet."

"In the dark?"

"I have excellent night vision."

"You had the door closed."

"I was chilly. Look, Officer . . ." Ellen checked the badge on his lapel. "Officer Flemm, without the proper paperwork, you had no right to enter my boat's cabin anyway. And any accusation that I'm 'not the same girlie' is pure hearsay and won't stand up in a court of law."

Officer Flemm pointed the nightstick at her, and Ellen got a close look at the dreadful hook. It wobbled for a moment as if it might catch her by the nostril. Then the policeman stabbed the hook straight down, into a can of sardines he held in his other hand. With deft wiggles of the hook, he cut open the lid. Ellen sighed with relief.

"The only court of law in Lach Lufless," said Officer Flemm, "is me." The can now open, he slurped the contents whole. "And I've got half a mind to haul you in for crimes against the community."

Pet had had enough. It snuck from the closet as if to repeat its hairy-ninja performance, but Officer Flemm noticed at once and flung the nightstick at the creature. The hook sunk into the floor mere inches from Pet's eye. Pet cowered.

"Dangerous animal off its leash," said Officer Flemm, wrenching the nightstick from the floor. "That's a major offense."

"That's my seeing-eye monkey," said Ellen. "It helps me see."

"I thought you had excellent vision."

"Only in the dark. Daylight, not so much."

Officer Flemm gave a low growl. He pulled out a notepad, scribbled on it, and tore off a sheet of paper, which he handed to Ellen.

"'Ticket for Suspicious Activity,'" Ellen read off the paper. "*That's* pretty vague. That will *never* stand up in . . . oh, yeah."

Officer Flemm gave her a gloating smile. "Get three of these tickets, and you face a terrible punishment—and I do mean terrible. We save our harshest penalties for troublemaking outsiders. So watch yourself, young lady. If I were you"—he leaned in so close, Ellen could smell his fishy breath—"I'd take this boat and sail back where you came from. Fast."

And with that he stabbed the hook into another can of sardines and left the cabin.

"Sheesh! A little . . . intense, don't you think, Pet?" said Ellen, emerging onto the deck and watching Flemm march back up the dock. "And not as gullible as I expected. Certainly not like the rubes in Nod's Limbs and Frøsthaven."

Pet pointed with a tendril to the buildings in the distance.

"Right. Keep moving. If we're lucky, Stephanie's already gotten three tickets, and as we speak, she's strung up by her pedicured toes."

9. Lacking Luflins

The road wound away from the docks, through the grassy heather and around a bend. Then, there it was: Lach Lufless. Or, at least, this is what Ellen had to assume. There was no sign welcoming them, as there was in Nod's Limbs and Frøsthaven. The only civic marker was another signpost with arrows, but this one was decidedly less helpful than the last.

TOWN HALL—ROUND THE BEND
PUBLIC PILLORY—OVER THERE
PAY TOILET—THAT WAY
BIG DAM—BACK AND BEYOND

The roadway improved from crumbling cobblestones to severely uneven cobblestones as it led them down the main thoroughfare of town. Unlike

Nod's Limbs, whose homes and stores were painted every color of the rainbow, or Frøsthaven, where all the buildings were whimsically carved from ice, these structures were as decrepit as the boats Ellen and Pet had just seen at the docks, as dismal as the mud that coated the cobblestones, as gray as the sky above.

Though it was not raining or uncomfortably cool, no one walked down the sidewalks or drove along the street. It was like a ghost town, and the only sound was the light breeze that whistled across the lake behind them. Pet shivered.

"I saw a movie like this once," said Ellen. "We should watch out for an army of the undead." Pet leaped up onto Ellen's shoulder and hid under one of her braids.

They started down the street, Ellen peering into windows for any sign of life, or unlife, if that was the case. But most of the shutters were drawn, and those windows that weren't shuttered only looked in on dark rooms. A couple of times Ellen looked up at the second and third stories, and could have sworn that eyes were peering down at her.

"This is creepy, Pet," she said. "If this is a town made nicey-nice by a nearby balm spring, where's

the welcoming committee? Where are the parades and the glitter and the inanely cheery townsfolk? For that matter, where are the townsfolk?"

As if in answer, a door slammed, and Ellen turned to see an elderly post-delivery woman exiting an old and rusting mail truck.

"Hello," said Ellen.

"Grmph," the woman replied, keeping her head down.

"I'm Ellen," said Ellen.

"Congratulations," the woman growled.

"Um, I'm new to town, and I was hoping you could help me."

"Do I look like a help desk?" said the woman. "Does this mailbag say *Customer Service*? In case your eyesight is as poor as your manners, I'll tell you that no, it does not." She continued to limp along, never looking Ellen in the eye.

"But I—"

"Now stop bothering me, young person. Can't you see I'm busy? Some of us have responsibilities to tend to, rather than playing in the street and bothering old ladies."

Ellen glanced at Pet. Over her lifetime she had encountered the most ridiculous and gullible people, and she was accustomed to using truth enhancement and subterfuge to deal with them.

She was not, however, prepared to handle a crotchety old woman who wouldn't let her get a sentence out.

"I thought Flemm was going to be the worst of them," Ellen said. "So far, he's the most pleasant."

Ellen heard a creaking sound and saw that it came from an iron sign swinging in the breeze across the street. *Stuffy's Luflins* it said in peeling paint. They entered.

It was a small grocer, and the look of the food soured even Ellen's less-than-picky taste buds. The produce stand held wilted heads of lettuce, dried-out carrots, rotting apples, and rancid parsnips. The shelves, lined with things like boxes of crackers and tins of sardines, were coated with dust, and a bitter smell permeated the air. Even the twins' kitchen at home, which was no center of culinary delight, wasn't this dismal.

Pet shivered slightly and jumped off Ellen's shoulder. It scurried outside and gave Ellen a "lots of luck, pal" salute before the door swung shut.

"Traitor," muttered Ellen. "It's just—*hack hack*—a little foul air."

Ellen made her way toward the counter at the back, taking care not to slip on the grimy floor. There, a man sat reading a newspaper, dressed in tattered overalls that looked as dirty as the rest of the store. After the encounter with the mail-woman, Ellen thought she might try a more direct approach.

"Hi there. I've just arrived in town, and what a lovely town it is. I don't suppose there are any festivals coming up? Parades? Contests?"

The man flipped the page of his newspaper. "Nope."

Ellen frowned. She was sure a multitude of celebrations would be a can't-miss sign they were near a balm spring. She had also been counting on scoring some free food scraps.

"Are you Stuffy?" she asked the man.

"Who's asking?"

"I am, obviously. What's a *luflin*?"

"That." He nodded in the direction of a cake plate on the counter. On it were dollops of something mushy and green; they looked a bit like piles of steamed spinach. Ellen realized that they were the source of the terrible smell.

"Local delicacy," the man said.

"Made from . . . ?"

"From seaweed growing in the lake," the man said. "Hey, now—you after my secret recipe?"

"Just making conversation," Ellen assured him. "You know who really likes conversing? That red-haired girl who's new in town. I'm sure you've seen her . . ."

"Why would you be so sure of that?" he snarled.

Ellen sighed. "Fine. Just tell me where the nearest inn is."

"Aren't any."

"No lodging?" asked Ellen incredulously.

"What use do we have for inns? We don't suffer visitors, and inns would only encourage them to come."

"Cripes," muttered Ellen. "You people are the crabbiest bunch of cranks I ever—"

Whoosh.

Ellen ducked just in time to miss the *luflin* that Stuffy threw at her. Another barrage of the delicacies spattered around her as she scampered out the door. A muffled shout came from the other side: "And stay out!"

10. Warmth and Hospitality

The sun was setting, or Ellen guessed it was from the darker gray pall of the sky. She hadn't actually *seen* the sun in days.

"Well, Pet, maybe we can find a barn or something to camp out in."

Ellen walked down the main street, Pet shuffling along at her side. Now and then they'd see a person or two, but always before Ellen could speak to them, they would slam their doors or close their curtains. Ellen kept getting the feeling that she was being watched or followed, but every time she turned around, no one was there.

Soon it began to drizzle. With no place to lay her head and nothing but a half bowl of *haggum* in her belly, Ellen choked back a cry of frustration. Pet wrapped a tendril around her hand and led her beneath the branches of a dismal yew. Though the evergreen was scraggly, it blocked most of the rain, and might even make passable bedding for the night.

Ellen drew her knees up under her chin and sulked in silence for some time.

"I'm worried, Pet," she said at last. "This doesn't seem like a balm spring kind of town. And Dahlia said Stephanie was leaving a trail for us to follow. Was this all some sort of trap? Has she led us astray and moved on to the *real* balm spring?"

Pet had no answer; instead it tried to take Ellen's mind off their predicament by providing a little light entertainment. It juggled chunks of cobblestone for her, even allowing itself to miss a few, which bonked on its eye. When that failed to get even a smile, Pet slumped next to her and traced amusing stick figures in the mud until the rain abated, while Ellen sang to pass the time:

Oh, Pet, what are we doing here?
These folks aren't filled with numbing cheer—
Lach Lufless seems far too austere
To claim a spring nearby.
But we found Dahlia, we found Nod,
New members of the zombie squad,
So, although it's very odd,
We can't have gone awry.

But Ellen was distracted by something else. In the ever-dimming light, she thought she saw movement behind a hedge just to the side of the tree.

"Shh, Pet," she whispered, perhaps deservedly, for Pet rarely made any noise at all. "Behind that bush. It could be Nod or Dahlia sneaking up on us. Why don't you do your best squirrel impression and find out who it is."

Pet nodded and ducked out from under the yew. By sticking out its tendrils in a fluffy tail, it did rather resemble a squirrel in the growing darkness.

It stole over to the hedge and poked around, as if looking for food. But just as it rounded the bush, a hand reached out and grabbed it by the scruff. Ellen leaped to her feet.

"You, hey you! I see you! You let my Pet go!"

She rounded the hedge, fists ready to pummel, and ran smack into a boy. They both fell to the ground, and Pet was able to wriggle free of the boy's grasp.

The boy brushed the dirt from his jacket and picked up his glasses, which had been knocked from his face.

He seemed about Ellen's age, but was smaller and frail-looking. His attire, however, was very grown up. He wore khaki slacks and a jacket and tie, and looked quite like he was on his way to a piano recital.

He stood up and offered a hand to Ellen to help her, but she ignored it and got up of her own accord.

"Who are you?" she demanded. "Why are you following us?"

"This muskrat is your pet?" asked the boy. "I didn't know they could be domesticated."

"You didn't answer my question," said Ellen. "Tell me who you are and why you're so interested in our business."

"My name is Archibald Tibbits," said the boy. "I am following you because I was ordered to do so."

"Who ordered you to? And why?"

"Question the first: the mayor. Question the second: because you are strangers."

"The hospitality in this town really isn't going to win any awards," said Ellen.

"No, it isn't," said Archibald. "Thank you for noticing. We do try our best."

"That was an *insult*," said Ellen. "Cripes, you all are deadly serious here."

Archibald blinked at Ellen. "Of course we are."

"Okay, Archie, it's been a real treat meeting you, but my Pet and I are just going to be on our way . . ." Ellen started off, and Archibald followed her.

"Where are you going?" he asked.

"Haven't figured that out yet, actually," said Ellen. "I hear you don't have any inns or hotels."

"That is correct."

"So I guess we'll leave. Maybe camp on the moors outside of town, then in the morning continue on to a friendlier place. You don't have to worry about us, Archie, we don't want to be here any more than you want us to."

"Pardon me, but I think that you are lying to me."

Ellen faked a shocked look. "Why would you say such a hurtful thing?"

"First off, you haven't any gear, which would make camping difficult and uncomfortable. Second, you were caught sneaking around on a boat that is not yours. Third, it has been reported that you are trying to gather information on someone, a fellow outsider, leading me to presume you are tracking this person—and failing. Which means you will stay to look for her, and in turn, I shall stay with you."

"Says who?"

"Says Mayor Tibbits," said Archibald. "It is my job to ensure that should you receive two more tickets, you face—"

"A terrible punishment. Yes, the copper told me," said Ellen. "I'm shaking in my footies." She paused. "*Tibbits.* Isn't that your last name?"

"It is. The mayor is my mother."

"I should have known. Mayoral children and I don't get along."

11. International Syrup Thieves

One of the first things Edgar learned as an apprentice monster hunter was that chewing a loonroot was the bitterest way to get a healthful meal in the backwoods. Instead, if one soaks the root in a pot of cold mountain stream water, and then adds the bark of a Brunswick birch (culled from the northwestern side of the tree) and a dash of yellow juniper moss, the result is a passable soup that is certainly no more foul than the gruel and porridge Edgar might have had at home.

Over the next day, Gristly Jefferson showed

Edgar the proper way to extract the juice from a nettleberry—as well as how to bandage the skin with strips of mushroom if one fumbles the job. Edgar learned how to clean a pocket can opener, how to extract a bramble from the ball of the foot, three ways to feast on ticks, two methods for setting broken bones, and how to use the hollow stalk of the Gershwin reed as a straw to suck dew off pinecones. (The reed also made a passable clarinet for tootling away the time. Edgar proved horrible at it.)

During this training Edgar examined each and every one of Gristly's traps that were set up around the mountain. He jiggered and reconfigured all of them to his own specifications, much to the woodsman's delight.

As Edgar tinkered, Gristly wandered off to do more scouting. Soon he called to Edgar: "Sally! Over here! Over here!"

Edgar followed the voice to where Gristly was, pointing at something in a soft patch of earth. Pressed into the ground was a footprint two hands wide and twice as long. Four distinct toe prints in front dug deep into the loam.

Edgar let out a low whistle. It was unlike any animal track he had ever seen—and it was huge.

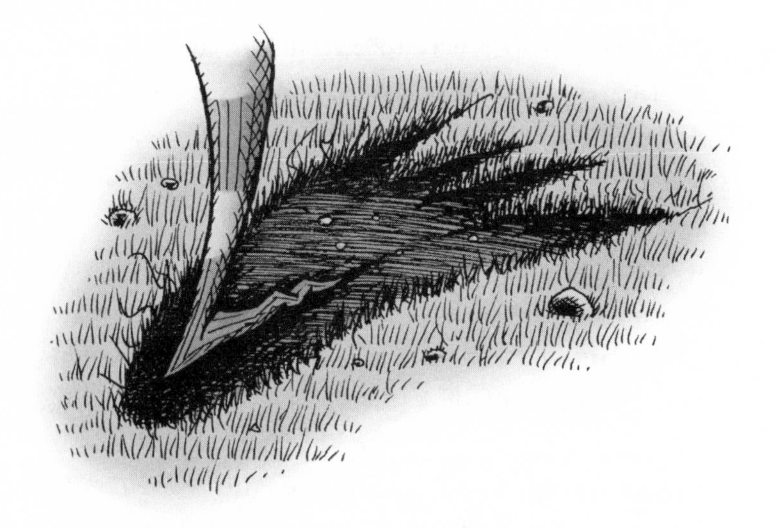

"Things like this keep me going on even the rainiest day," Gristly said in a faraway voice. "I remember my first one. I was town librarian in Cougar Falls, as upstanding a citizen as they come. Then one day I came up here to collect specimens for our *Take a Likin' to Lichen* exhibit, and that's when I found the tracks. Two huge ones just like this beauty."

"What'd you do?" asked Edgar.

"I followed them, of course. All day and all night, till I thought I had him. I could hear faint sounds of movement through the forest, always just ahead of me. I had my camera for the shot of a lifetime. There had been legends in Cougar Falls for years about the Squatch, but everyone figured they were just children's stories. No one had ever been able to prove the thing was real—but I was going to change that."

"Did you get the shot?"

"The Squatch . . . well, it got the drop on me. I never got a good look at it—something hit me on the head, knocked me out cold. When I finally woke up, my camera was all busted up." Gristly stroked his beard and sighed.

"And you've been out here ever since?"

"Not exactly. I went back to town, told them what I'd seen—that the Squatch was real, that it might be dangerous, that we should send out a search party and learn more about it. But they hushed me up. Said the tourists would stop coming if folks thought a 'silly old myth' was actually real. So they shunned me—and I shunned them. Been up here for almost ten years trying to prove them wrong."

The next morning, after Edgar had reworked the final trap, he clapped his mushroom-wrapped hands and took a deep breath of crisp hill-country air.

"Well, I'm a new man, Gris," he said. "I'm all

woodsy and outdoorsy now. Yes, sir, one hundred percent rugged. Now . . . what's the fastest way to find this Footsie creature?"

"Oh, we won't find him. He'll find us," said Gristly. "Ol' Footsie is as shy as he is savage. Wants to be left alone."

"But there must be a place where most of your sightings happen," said Edgar. "Some spot rumored to be its hideout? Anything?"

"No, the Squatch chooses when to show himself and to whom, which is why the most important skill of a monster hunter is *patience*," said Gristly. "In fact, our next lesson is about how to lie perfectly still for up to three weeks at a time."

Edgar sighed, when a twig snapped in the distance.

"What's that you said about patience?" he asked quietly. Another branch snapped, and they could hear a light crackle of dry leaves.

"Footsie!" whispered Gristly Jefferson. "Quick, get to cover!"

The two hunters dove behind a bush and held their breath. The sound of footfalls came closer and closer, crunching through leaves and dry twigs.

"Wait just a northwoods second," whispered

Gristly Jefferson. "The Squatch would never make so much racket . . ."

A voice called out, "Hoo-ee! This barrel is heavier than an elephant tusk with the elephant attached."

"Gonzalo!" whispered Edgar.

"I think we missed the path back to the rendezvous point, Gonzalo." It was Phoebe's small voice. "Maybe we should go back, uh, *this* way."

"If you say so, little lady," said Gonzalo. "Just get me back before I bust a gut. Then Imogen will have to haul me out of here in a bucket."

"What the blazes is going on out there?" said Gristly softly. "These don't sound like hikers." He stood to get a better look.

Edgar could see through a gap in the branches, and indeed it was Gonzalo and Phoebe approaching. Imogen, Mab, and Merrick were nowhere to be seen. Though not much older than Edgar, the cowboy clown was extremely large and strong for his age. Now his thick arms were wrapped around a broad barrel that had a dense amber fluid dripping down its sides. The balm that Edgar knew from Nod's Limbs was white, but his foray into the Arctic had taught him that the mysterious substance could come in other colors, such as the light blue kind from the Black Diamond Glacier.

"That's balm, I know it!" Edgar whispered to himself.

"Well, duh," he responded back.

Gristly Jefferson was whispering something quite different, however.

"That's maple syrup, I know it!" He seized Edgar's elbow. "Stay here, Sally. We've got some maple poachers in our woods—probably running an illegal syrup operation. They could be desperate and dangerous. Let me handle them."

Edgar seized him as he was about to run off. "No! They'll lead us to the others!"

"What?" asked Gristly Jefferson.

"Er, well, these illegal syrup operations aren't small-time, you know," said Edgar. "There must be others waiting for them back at their rendezvous point. Let's follow!"

"Hmm. Maybe you're right, Sally. But still, let me deal with these poachers. You'd be in over your head with them."

"In over my head, huh?" said Edgar. "Gris, watch this."

As Gonzalo and Phoebe crunched away through

the fallen leaves, Edgar grabbed a short copper tube and a threepenny nail from his satchel. With a deft gesture, he slipped the nail in the tube, aimed the tube at the barrel, and blew into one end. The nail shot out and struck the barrel with a soft *tack*.

"What was that about?" asked Gristly Jefferson.

"*That* was about brilliance. That barrel will leak, and we'll have a trail to follow," said Edgar. "Plus, you can't steal what your barrel can't hold," he murmured to himself.

"Brilliant thwarting, Edgar," he whispered.

"Thanks, Edgar," he said in return.

But the woodsman was unimpressed. "Aw, Sally. It's called *tracking*. We follow the signs they leave behind *naturally* as they pass. I guess that's your next lesson."

12. Sir Salvatore Tells the Truth

As Edgar and Gristly tiptoed through the brush on the trail of Gonzalo and Phoebe, they spotted little globs of amber balm on the bed of leaves and pine needles. These started out as beads no bigger than dewdrops, but soon the dollops grew to the size of

New Pakatchaloosa nickels. Edgar picked up a glob of the goop and rubbed it between his mushroom-bandaged fingers.

"Strange," said Gristly Jefferson, watching over Edgar's shoulder. "Maple sap is usually runny. And it doesn't smell this peculiar. And come to think of it, this isn't even sap season. Maybe this isn't maple at all—"

"What? Oh, sure it is," said Edgar. "This is just, uh, the unique product of the rare *blood maple*."

"A blood maple, you say?" Gristly whistled softly. "Well, that *must* be rare. I've never heard of it . . . and, you know, *I live in a forest*." He fixed his eyes on Edgar, who gulped.

The last thing Edgar wanted was to bring Gristly Jefferson in on the secret of the balm. He had long ago learned the legend of Mad Duke Disease—the intense greed that infects those who learn of the balm's life-extending power. Such greed had led to wars in centuries past, and it was this very thing the Heimertz circus had pledged to prevent. Edgar had no desire to see yet another balm-mad lunatic interfere in his quest.

The woodsman snorted. "Sally, you know more than you're saying."

"Me? No, I'm just an apprentice monster hunter—"

"Haw! If that's all you are, I'll eat my tuque."

"Your what?"

"My *hat*, kid, my *hat*. I'm saying I've got my eye on you." Gristly Jefferson tapped a finger under his eye. "I don't know what's going on in these woods, but I didn't survive out here this long by being easily fooled."

Edgar felt a bead of sweat form on his brow. "Whatever you say, Gristly. I just want to stop some poachers."

Gristly Jefferson took a long look at Edgar before he continued. "All right, then. I'm going to shinny up this cedar and see where they're going. Stay put, got it?"

As the woodsman climbed the tree, Edgar paced and mumbled to himself.

"I can't have him fouling up a covert operation." He eyed a length of rope protruding from his satchel. "I should lash him to the tree trunk with a quick Shanghai slipknot and be done with him."

"Not so fast, Edgar," he replied to himself. "Can you really take all five Midway Irregulars by yourself? Wouldn't it be smarter to employ the extra muscle?"

"Now, self, this is no time to start doubting me!" Edgar almost yelled. Gristly Jefferson hushed him from up in the tree.

Edgar sighed.

"Gristly finding out about the balm couldn't possibly be worse than Stephanie getting her hands on all of it," he muttered. "I have to stop the Irregulars at all costs."

"Right, then. No Shanghai slipknots."

Gristly Jefferson slid down the trunk of the cedar and landed with a thud next to Edgar. "There's three of them in the Pineycone Pocket, waiting for the two with the barrel. Bad news for us."

"Why? What's the Pineycone Pocket?"

"It's a grove of pines in the middle of Footwood Forest. See, most of the trees here are leafy, and there's lots of bracken, which is good for hiding in. In the Pineycone Pocket, the trees are barer and stand farther apart. Less coverage. It'll be hard for us to sneak up on them." Gristly scratched his beard. "They've got four more barrels sitting down there too."

"Gristly, listen," interrupted Edgar. "I know these guys. They're the circus folk I was looking for."

"Yeah, I know, Sally," said Gristly Jefferson. "Two of them were juggling bowling pins, and the other is wearing a *top hat*, for crying out loud. Carnies for sure."

"That—that's right. Look, these guys aren't just dangerous, they're tricky. They're under the spell of something really powerful, something made from *this*," he said, holding up a glob of balm. "And they'll fight to protect it. I have the antidote, but the thing is, I may not be able to administer it by myself. I think—I think I need your help."

"Well, I'll be," said Gristly Jefferson. "Sir Salvatore Shipsailington finally tells me the truth."

"Another thing. My name is really—"

"Edgar," said Gristly. "I know. It's what you say when you're talking to yourself. So, how about we work together to bag these savage zombie clowns, eh, Sally?"

13. The World's Weirdest Lunchtime

Two innocent shrubs crept from tree to tree into the Pineycone Pocket. Gristly had been right: The firs growing here were much sparser than the deciduous trees that made up most of the forest. Edgar spotted the Irregulars from far off, gathered in a clearing around a fallen pine, but that meant they could see him just as easily if he wasn't careful. The silently stalking Edgar carried a crooked fishhook in one hand, and Gristly a fishing reel. The two were connected by a single strand of nylon filament that Edgar had found in his satchel.

"Ellen would have called this plan mad," Edgar said to himself through the pain of cramped muscles. "Ha! Would a madman have been so wise as this?"

The two shrubs inched to within earshot of the Midway Irregulars. Phoebe was helping Mab and Merrick, the brother and sister acrobats, rustle up a lunch of baked beans over a small camp stove, while future ringmaster Imogen was inspecting their most recent haul. Gonzalo, however, was positioned perfectly. He sat slightly off to the side on the fallen pine, whittling a Ferris wheel from a bar of soap.

Gonzalo was not the craftiest of their targets, but he was easily the strongest. Edgar thought it best to turn him first, but he was far too large for Edgar's makeshift nets. Therefore, it was up to Gristly to contain him long enough for Edgar to feed him the antidote. But all this hinged on luring Gonzalo away from the group. When Edgar had crept to within a yard of his target, he readied his fishhook between pinched fingers and took aim. He took a deep breath and—

"Gonzalo?" called Imogen. "Did you do this on purpose?"

Gonzalo hopped to his feet.

"Rats," breathed Edgar as Gonzalo ran over to the balm-filled barrels, where Imogen stood.

"Great gully washers!" exclaimed the cowboy. "This barrel's empty!"

"Look, it had a leak," said Mab, the acrobat.

"From a nail hole!" said her brother Merrick.

"I didn't know," said Gonzalo. "It got lighter as we went, but I just thought I was getting stronger!"

"How did a nail get in there in the middle of the wilderness?" asked Imogen. Edgar ducked down low as she removed her ringmaster's top hat and placed it on the log right above him.

"Maybe the barrel was like that when it was shipped to Cougar Falls," said Merrick. "Miss Stephanie makes mistakes too, doesn't she?"

The Irregulars fell silent at this, as if something were nagging at them.

"I . . . I think we should eat lunch," said Phoebe. "Remember what Miss Stephanie said about eating on time every day . . ."

The Midway Irregulars nodded eagerly at this, as if coming out of a trance.

"Or falling back *into* one," Edgar noted to himself. He watched Gonzalo fill five tin cups from a large canteen, hand them around, then take his seat back on the log, a mere foot from where Edgar lay hidden. Edgar again slithered slowly toward him.

The Irregulars ate their beans with little gusto, like they had not much appetite, and Edgar saw for the first time how dead their eyes looked. As they chewed the beans, Mab pulled out a battered tape recorder.

"Time for our meal-time motivational message from Miss Stephanie," she said.

"Ten-hut, circus scum!" Stephanie Knightleigh's voice barked out of the tape player. "I'm here to tell you once again of your missions. Mission one is to get the balm from Cougar Falls. At least four full barrels."

"Mission accomplished," said the Irregulars in unison.

"Mission two," said Stephanie. "Find the beast's

lair and destroy it, but I want the beast alive. He's valuable to me."

"Mission unresolved," said the Irregulars.

"Once you have accomplished these two things, sit tight at the rendezvous point until you receive further instructions," said Stephanie. "Don't forget the rules. Rule one: If you see Edgar and/or Ellen, stop them any way you can. Edgar and Ellen are the enemy. Rule two: Always take your medicine at meal times!"

"Bottoms up," said the Irregulars, and they quaffed their drinks. It apparently was not tasty, for they gagged as the stuff went down, but they soon shook it off and smiled their Heimertz family smiles once again.

Inside his shrubby disguise, Edgar shook his head. "So that's how she's keeping them under her spell." He was inches away from Gonzalo now. Just a little further . . .

"Rule three: No thinking for yourselves. Now, remember, soldiers," said Stephanie, "the boss and I are counting on you. If you obey us, you will be rewarded beyond your wildest dreams. So don't screw this up!"

"We won't!" piped the Irregulars.

"That's the spirit," continued Stephanie. "Now, Mob, rewind this tape and play it at the next meal."

"Oh right, that's me," said Mab. "I keep forgetting my name's Mob!" She picked up the tape player and hit REWIND.

"The boss?" Edgar whispered, halting his advance. "Who is Stephanie working with *now*?"

In the Arctic it had been the mad hermit Uta Glögg, who assisted Stephanie in her schemes, but who could be her accomplice in these hills?

Edgar grunted. "Gristly qualifies as a mad hermit, all right, but he seems pretty harmless. So who . . . ? Well, let's engage Operation: Hat's Off and find out."

As Gonzalo was scraping the last of his beans from his bowl, Edgar extended his hand again and flicked the little fishhook. It landed with a soft *tap* on the brim of the cowboy's hat. All Gristly would have to do is give the fishing reel a swift yank to set the hook in the felt, and Gonzalo's hat would fly into the woods on a mysterious forest "wind." Edgar lifted his hand to give the go signal to Gristly.

Whoomph!

A cloud of smoke exploded in the center of the clearing. The Irregulars let out astonished cries, and Gonzalo tumbled backward off the log, nearly flattening Edgar. Tendrils of smoke slithered ominously from the burst, and a figure emerged from the swirling smoke: a tall man in a garish red tuxedo. He swept his cape with a dramatic flourish and took a bow to the applause of the Midway Irregulars.

"And *that* is how the best showmen make an entrance," he said.

It was the very last person Edgar had ever expected to see.

"Impossible," he said.

14. The Angry Shrub

"Boss!" cried Imogen. "We weren't expecting you!"

"That's the first rule of showmanship: Never do the expected," said Ormond the Impossible.

"Boy howdy, that's what I call a showstopper!" enthused Gonzalo as he picked up his hat. The fishhook fell harmlessly to the forest floor.

Edgar hardly noticed Gonzalo anymore. The last time he saw Ormond Heimertz, the escapist extraordinaire was delivering what was expected to be the greatest performance of his life. But before it was over, the big top of the Heimertz Family Circus collapsed, and everyone believed that Ormond had died in the wreckage. But Edgar knew what really happened. It was all a scam Ormond had orchestrated to get rich and win freedom from the circus, and in the process he cheated the twins out of their own house.

Oh, and he had contrived to have much of the blame for the collapsed tent placed on Ellen and her brother—the trusting, fawning apprentice to Ormond the Impossible.

"You backstabbing old scoundrel," whispered Edgar. "We've got a score to settle."

He nearly charged headlong into the grove to tackle his former mentor. But then he realized what Ormond's appearance meant: Not only was this one more variable to wrangle with, this was *Ormond the Impossible*. He may have been far less skilled than Edgar had given him credit for (Edgar was crushed to find that Ormond's shackles were fakes); nonetheless, he was still a cunning and clever opponent.

"I see you've completed your mission," said Ormond. "Five full barrels of the precious stuff. Hark—what's this? This barrel is almost empty! Have you layabouts been sandbagging?"

"It's just a leaky barrel, Boss," said Imogen. "We'll get it patched and refill it this afternoon. Besides, Miss Stephanie said we only needed four barrels."

"Is she running this business?" Ormond demanded. "Five barrels—I insist on it."

"When does business begin?" asked Merrick.

"It has already!" said Ormond. "I have recently contacted a few select figures in positions of power around the globe. They were skeptical of my claims, of course, but once I made a small demonstration, the bidding began. The second rule of showmanship, children: Always leave them wanting more. Soon, as more people discover I've bottled the fountain of youth, the prices will sail beyond *astronomical.*"

"Good for you, Boss!" said Phoebe. "We'll be rich!"

"Yes, I will," said Ormond. "Laden with more lucre than the fullest Pharaoh's tomb."

"And so will we!" cheered Phoebe.

"Well, you'll be comfortable," said Ormond. "But, sweet Phoebe, my little insect trainer, how can I get rich if I don't have enough balm to sell? You must fix that barrel and get me more at once."

"This is just about money? *Mere common crookery?*" breathed Edgar. "They'll give the *whole world* Mad Duke Disease. Nod was right to be paranoid."

Edgar noticed that Gristly's shrub had begun to rustle. Edgar could only guess that the woodsman was wondering just what he had stumbled upon. Edgar nearly revealed himself as he wiggled his branches this way and that to warn Gristly to stay put.

"Keep still, blast you!" he mouthed.

Phoebe raised her hand. Ormond sighed, exasperated.

"What is it, Phoebe?"

"Well, we can get the balm in a jiffy, but the

ithune may take a little longer. This is the one they call Ol' Footsie, and if you remember, circus lore says it's particularly tricky."

"What does that hairy *ithune* have to do with anything?" said Ormond. "If it gives you any trouble, dispatch it at once. Steal all its balm and let it starve for all I care."

"But Miss Stephanie said we should capture it," said Phoebe.

Ormond glowered. "What use has she for the smelly beast? No, I say if it troubles you, crack it over the head with a—"

"*Just stop right there, pal!*" The command came from the tall bush striding into the clearing.

"You fool!" hissed Edgar quietly. "You've ruined everything!"

Gristly Jefferson stomped forward fiercely as he ripped his branches off and shook them at Ormond. "First, you people want to steal this—this *whatever* from my woods, and now you think you can murder Ol' Footsie? You've got another think coming!"

It was over almost before Ormond's fingers had finished snapping. The Irregulars sprang into action so quickly, it was like they were performing a well-rehearsed circus routine. Imogen swept her leg under Gristly Jefferson, causing his knees to buckle. As Gristly fell on his rump, Gonzalo sent a lasso over him, cinching the woodsman's elbows to his ribs. Mab and Merrick finished the job with a barrage of bowling pins at Gristly's head and chest, and he was knocked unconscious before he could begin to fight back.

A moment later he was gagged, wrapped tighter than a fly in a spider web, and hoisted into the treetops for safekeeping.

"A wolf in shrub's clothing," said Ormond. "There could be more. Fan out."

The Midway Irregulars exploded forth from the Pineycone Pocket. Had Edgar not already instinctively scuttled up the trunk of a pine, Merrick would have discovered him immediately. But tucked into the crook of a knobby limb, he blended in perfectly with the forest canopy.

Ormond lingered at the campsite, stroking his chin theatrically. "How much did you overhear, I wonder?" he said to the suspended body of Gristly Jefferson. He checked his pocket watch. "Hang it all, I have another fifteen meetings in town before the day's end. Selling the fountain of youth is such tedious business. Your interrogation will have to wait, I'm afraid, until tomorrow morning. You'll be comfortable here through the night, won't you?"

Chuckling, Ormond the Impossible strolled away from the pine grove, leaving the Midway Irregulars to their work.

Edgar found himself alone again in the wood with no plan, no partner, and no clue what to do next. He glared at Gristly Jefferson strung up in the tree and began to sing:

You fool! You dunce! You sad buffoon!
You nincompoop! You plaid-clad loon!
Hope you enjoy that rope cocoon—
I'll leave you there to swing.
Besides, an ugly head has reared,
The worst of all I once revered—
Ormond. Ormond has reappeared.
This changes everything.

15. The Walk Side of the Sidewalk

Ellen tried countless ways to shake Archibald—assuring him over and over again that she and Pet meant no harm, that they were not escaped criminals, that they were decent, law-abiding folk—but whether Archibald believed this or not, he refused to leave her side as they walked down the streets of Lach Lufless.

"What you say may be true, and it may not," he said. "Why you are here is of no concern to me. I am to chaperone you until you leave. And that is that."

"Oh, all right already," said Ellen. "But if you're going to be my travel buddy, you have to answer my questions."

"What would you like to know?"

"A friend of mine was supposed to meet me here, and I've been trying to find her. Red hair, yells a lot."

"No one new has come to town except for you."

"*Now* who's lying?" Ellen said. "Officer Flim-flam said he saw a girl who didn't look like me on that speedboat."

"Indeed. And this girl has not come to town. *Ipso facto*, I have not lied."

"Okay, okay. No need for French," said Ellen.

"Latin."

"Whatever," said Ellen. "Anyway, if my, uh, friend is staying outside of the town proper, I suppose I should head back to the docks and wait for her."

"As long as we don't loiter, that would be acceptable," said Archibald as he gestured toward a street that would lead them back to the lake.

Ellen shook her head. "So what's with Lach Lufless anyway? Why are you all so . . . lacking?"

"Lacking what?"

"Cheer. Good humor. Warmth toward your fellow man."

"I do not understand what you mean, Ellen," said Archibald. "We are as cheerful as we need to be. Why be happier or sadder than necessary?"

"Have you ever considered that you might be a robot?" said Ellen.

"Of course not. Lifelike robotic replicas are decades away, maybe more."

"I'm serious. This town has no festivals, no holidays, no parades—not even the odd tea party?"

"Such things tend to interrupt the workday," said Archibald, "and that would certainly not be something to celebrate."

"It's like the anti-Nod's Limbs," Ellen muttered. "We *can't* be near a balm spring."

"What's that?" asked Archibald.

"It's nothing. Tell me, does a circus ever come through town? The Heimertz Family Circus?"

Archibald took a few seconds to respond. "Yes, they show up every few years."

"Aha!" said Ellen. "So where do they set up camp?"

"Well, outside town limits," said Archibald. "They aren't allowed inside Lach Lufless. Too distracting. But they keep coming back even though no one goes to their circus."

"No one goes?"

Archibald grimaced, showing his first real emotion since Ellen had met him.

"We find it best to . . . engage with them as little as possible," he said. "Tedra Heimertz comes to town from time to time for groceries, of course, but when her family visits, we keep them all at a safe distance." Archibald noticed Ellen's dropped jaw. "What's the matter?"

"Did you say 'Tedra Heimertz?'" she asked. "A Heimertz lives here?"

"Yes. For dozens of years."

Ellen rubbed her hands together.

"I know the Heimertz family, and I'm sure Tedra would be horrified if I didn't stop by and say hello. Come to think of it, that might be where my friend went too."

"You—you want to go all the way out there?" asked Archibald. "It's a good way round the lake."

"It's not like I have a place to stay in town, is it?" said Ellen. "Lead on, dear Archie, lead on. That is, unless you want to just give me directions and head on home. It's getting late, and I'm sure your mother, the mayor, wants you back for dinner. Mmm, dinner." Ellen's stomach grumbled at her.

"No, I will take you there," said Archibald. "It's this way." He led them down a side street. On the way they passed a familiar policeman standing by a streetlamp.

"You again!" said Ellen. "Are you following me?"

"Hello, Archibald," said Officer Flemm, nodding at the mayoral son. "Keeping odd company, aren't we?"

"Mother's orders."

"Rightly so," Officer Flemm replied, pulling out a notepad. He scribbled on it, tore off the sheet, and handed it to Ellen.

"Another ticket?" she cried. "I'm just standing here! With the mayor's son! What's suspicious about that?"

"Nothing at all," said Officer Flemm. "This is a

charge for walking on the wrong side of the sidewalk." He pointed at the ground, and sure enough, a line was painted down the center. Ellen hadn't paid any attention to it. "'Walk on the left, traffic is deft; walk on the right, earn yourself spite.'"

"But there was no one else on the sidewalk!" fumed Ellen.

"And thank goodness! What if there had been? Bumping elbows and I don't know what else! We don't take kindly to irresponsible walking here in Lach Lufless," huffed Officer Flemm.

"This is ridiculous," said Ellen. "I—"

"No, this is your second ticket, young miss," said the officer. "You're lucky I don't give you a third for that ugly seeing-eye beast." Pet puffed up its hair in indignation. "You hear me? One more ticket and—"

"A terrible punishment. I got it, I got it," said Ellen, wadding up the ticket in her fist.

Archibald shook hands with the officer, and he, Ellen, and Pet continued down the sidewalk, single-file.

16. Circus Hospitality

"Where were you on that one, Archie?" said Ellen when they'd passed out of earshot of the policeman.

"I was standing to your left," said Archibald.

"I mean, why didn't you tell me about the stupid sidewalk rule?"

"You didn't ask. It's not my fault you didn't study our laws before you came here."

"Infuriating fiend!" said Ellen, and they walked the rest of the way in silence.

They filed along the lake for almost an hour, and it was fully dark by the time they arrived at a small cottage overlooking the shore. Ellen strode up to the dark house and knocked on the door. They waited, but no one answered.

"No one's home," said Archie. "Let's go."

"You don't know much about the Heimertzes, do you?" asked Ellen.

"Thankfully, no," said Archibald.

"Well, they're circus folk, and they live by circus rules. They have their own absurd laws, if you will. And one of them is that if a friend pops by, they are always allowed to stay, even if the host isn't home."

"That doesn't sound very likely," said Archibald.

"Perhaps not to a Lach Luflesser," said Ellen, "but not everyone in the world shares your view on visitors. If you knew anything about circuses, you'd know I was right."

Archibald considered this.

"Do you know where the key to the house is?"

"Ah, that's the beauty of it," said Ellen. She held Pet up to the doorknob. "You're looking at the master of the Stock Maiden 900."

"Is that an automobile race?" asked Archibald.

After another deft demonstration of follicular finesse, Pet turned the newly unlocked knob. Ellen could not find a light switch, but after a quick sweep of the room, Pet returned with a gas lamp and matches. Ellen lit the lamp, and they took in their surroundings.

Ellen, Archibald, and Pet were in a small kitchen adjacent to an even smaller bedroom, and this was the extent of the house. Dust covered everything, and a chair by the kitchen table was knocked over. A quick search determined there was no food in the icebox or clothes in the closet.

"Perhaps the Heimertz woman moved away," said Archibald.

"Or perhaps she met with some foul play," said Ellen. "Either way, we're staying here until I figure out what's happened to her."

"Very well," said Archibald. "I cannot prove that you aren't her friend, or that you aren't welcome here. But as long as you're staying, so am I."

"Fine," said Ellen, stretching out on the lumpy sofa. "You get the floor."

17. Gone Swimming

Ellen was so exhausted from her travels that she didn't rise until mid-morning. Now she was famished, having eaten nothing since the half bowl of ram-bladder soup the previous day.

The simple kitchen held nothing but a cast-iron stove and a small pantry with a single tin of beans.

"Good for your heart," sighed Ellen. "Well, let's fire up this stove and split the can for breakfast.

Archie, make yourself useful and go get some firewood."

"I go wherever you go," Archibald replied, rising from his makeshift bed on the kitchen floor.

"Oh, all right," groaned Ellen, and she and Archibald went to search for bracken and kindling.

Pet found a rickety shed that they had not noticed the night before. It crept through a chink in the wall to explore. A moment later it reappeared and frantically swished its tendrils until Ellen looked up. It beckoned for her to come over.

"That's definitely Heimertz construction," said Ellen as she approached the shed. "Looks just like the one Ronan used to live in." She yanked the door open. Archibald peered over her shoulder.

Like the closet on the boat, the shed was filled with diving equipment. Only this was not the high-tech kind Ellen and Pet had stumbled upon earlier. These suits were old-timey, made of worn canvas and iron, with giant globe helmets that made them look more like space suits than scuba gear. Pet hopped up and down excitedly.

"I know, Pet, I know," said Ellen. "So Tedra is a diver. And Stephanie had diving equipment and all that sonar stuff." She gazed out at the lake, the

water almost disturbingly calm in the chilly morning air. "It looks peaceful enough, but I wonder if there's something down there worth seeing."

"Dive in the lake?" asked Archibald. "You can't be serious."

"Serious as a cuckoo wasp attack," said Ellen. "Why not? The equipment's here. It's a lovely day. Sort of. Doesn't this place ever get any sun?"

"N-no one goes in the lake," said Archibald.

"Sharks? Giant squid?"

"Don't be ridiculous. It's freshwater."

"So what, then?"

"It's not . . . safe," said Archibald, shifting from one foot to the other.

"Like that's ever bothered me before," said Ellen. "Come on, let's get that firewood, then you can educate me on water safety, Lach Lufless-style."

After a breakfast of beans and more berries, which was not near enough to satisfy Ellen's hunger, Ellen returned to the shed and put on a scuba suit over her pajamas.

"You really are going in there?" asked Archibald.

"Of course."

"But why?"

"What can I say, I'm a nut for the water," said Ellen as she donned her suit.

"This lake is not something to be taken lightly," clucked Archibald. "It was not created to be enjoyed."

"Oh, really? And what was it created for?"

"To be avoided! Centuries ago, these lands were wild and chaotic places," said Archibald. "Clans of families battled one another incessantly. Nothing but disharmony and discord. Then our town founder, Angus MacLuff, dammed up the Spurtlenathy River, forming a lake that brought order to the region."

"What? How could a lake do that?"

"By keeping all those other brawlers away from us," said Archibald. "The lake was too big to cross, and Clan MacLuff could live in peace. That is why we respect the lake so."

"That's a stupid story," said Ellen. "Why don't people just go for a splash?"

"Swimming is discouraged, as there are far safer and more efficient ways to enjoy oneself," said Archibald. "For example, staying home to watch paint dry."

"I see. Well, that's more fun than I can handle, Archie," said Ellen. "I'll just stick to something simple, like scuba diving."

"Then I'm going too." Archibald sighed. "I promised Mother I would stay by your side, and I shall."

Pet jumped up and down next to Ellen's feet.

"Yes, you can come too, Pet," said Ellen, "though I think you'll just need the helmet." She plopped

Pet inside one of the globelike helmets—it actually made a cozy submersible for the little hairball—then attached the air hose to the top. She did the same for herself, and Archibald followed suit.

"Why are these wired for radio communication?" asked Archibald as he slipped on his helmet. His voice rang out of scratchy speakers inside the other helmets.

"Maybe so everyone can hear you scream," replied Ellen.

Archibald paled.

They waded into the lake until the water was above their heads. It was beyond dark even just inches below the surface, and Ellen turned on the underwater flashlight they had found with the suits. Even then, the light illuminated only about a foot in front of them, revealing dark swirls and rotten clumps of seaweed floating about.

They swam toward the middle of the lake—that is, Ellen and Archibald swam. Pet had to be tethered to Ellen, and it bobbed along next to her in the helmet. They spied no fish, no animals of any kind, though Ellen imagined there could be a giant man-eating eel in front of them and they'd never see it until they were halfway into its belly.

"According to this gauge in my helmet, we're thirty-five feet below the surface," said Ellen into her microphone.

"That's thirty-five feet deeper than any Lach Luflesser has ever gone," said Archibald. "Except Dennis 'Daredevil' Douglass."

"How deep did he go?" asked Ellen.

"Seeing as how he never came up, we assume he went all the way."

They swam in silence for a while after that.

Then something brushed past Ellen's ankle, and she felt something grab her flipper. She gasped and shined her flashlight at her attacker.

What had hold of her flipper might have been that man-eating eel, she feared—it certainly had a nasty mouth full of teeth—but the head was flat and eyeless, and its long, stringy body trailed deep into the lake.

Then Ellen noticed something truly odd: The body had *leaves*.

18. *Nepenthes Aquatis*

"*Nepenthes* plants!" cried Ellen. She gently pulled herself from the plant's jaws and shone the flashlight around her. The chomping mouth wasn't alone—little snapping heads writhed into view all around them. It was as if they were just drooling for a bite of trespassers.

Archie stifled a yell and swam higher, but Ellen drifted closer for a better look at those vicious jaws. Though they were definitely a different subspecies, Ellen knew they belonged to the same family of plants as her very own Morella, and Madame Dahlia's Gustav, and the *Nepenthes arcticus* she and Edgar had found in the Black Diamond Glacier at Frøsthaven.

Ellen held out her gloved hand to one of the mouths, which chomped down hard on her fingers. Rather than jerking her hand away, she let the plant gnaw while she patted it happily. Several more specimens drifted closer and joined the munching frenzy on Ellen's hand. She scratched a few lovingly on their heads.

"What a bunch of sweeties," she said. "*Nepenthes* always grow near a balm spring, Pet! We must be close. The spring is *in the lake*!"

Pet nodded its eyeball, glancing nervously at the hungry plants. It was protected by the helmet, but it had been bitten by one of these before, and it knew from recent memory that *Nepenthes* seeds were poisonous to its kind.

"Archie, what do you know about these plants?" Ellen asked as they swam just above the reach of the lunging mouths.

"Th-they're snagglestalks!" said Archibald. "We make *luflins* out of them—or, at least, the lifeless ones that wash up on shore. I had no idea they could, ah, gnash quite like this."

"*Luflins*? Ugh, I've had the pleasure of smelling them," said Ellen.

"Quite a popular dessert," said Archibald. "Who knew it came from such a disagreeable plant?"

"These beauties aren't disagreeable!" snapped Ellen. "They're just misunderstood."

"Why are you letting them harm your hand that way?"

"Oh, this doesn't hurt . . . much," said Ellen. "They're just showing affection. See, the *Nepenthes* has a rare—"

Something whipped past Ellen, nearly knocking the flashlight from her hands.

"Pet, was that you?" she demanded, but Pet was floating next to her, and it shook its eye no.

"Ack!" cried Archibald behind them. "Something just hit me in the stomach. It was like a . . a tentacle!"

"I thought you said there weren't squid in here."

"There aren't. It can't be true. There are no such things as monsters."

"Monsters? Who said anything about monsters?" Ellen whipped the flashlight back and forth, but saw only the plants and darkness.

"I-it's all a lie. It isn't true. The circus kids made it up to sc-scare me when I was little." Archibald was practically hyperventilating in his helmet.

"Slow down, Archie," said Ellen, grabbing him by the shoulders. "Breathe deeply. Now, tell me, what did the circus kids say exactly?"

"They told me about the . . . the Lufless Monster that lives in the lake. It has scales that knives can't pierce, and a long tail that can strangle you. But the thing that kills you is . . . is . . . the deadly gaze of its single evil eye." At this he glanced at Pet, who in turn looked at Ellen.

"I was afraid you were going to say that," said Ellen. "Swim! Swim for it! We have to get out of here *now*!"

Flapping their flippers as fast as they could, the two children swam toward the surface.

Ellen thought she could see the water lightening, the gray of the sky above, and then something wrapped around her leg. It pulled her down, down, down into the depths of the water, away from light and safety.

"Archie, help! Help me!" she called out, but Archibald did not respond. Pet bobbled next to her, egging her forward with its tendrils. Ellen clawed at the thing clutching her leg, but its grip was viselike.

Down and down it dragged her, until she was sure she would smack against the bottom at any moment. And then, abruptly, it let go.

Ellen and Pet hung suspended in the water, scarcely daring to breathe. Ellen swung the flashlight around, but the monster was nowhere to be seen. And then she felt a swish as something rushed past her, and there it was, the thing she had been dreading.

The creature before them was long and slender, even longer than Yehti, the beast of the arctic. The main body was a gelatinous mass covered in hair like a platypus's, and from this hung swaths of longer tresses. These tendrils swirled about in thick strands as if half a dozen octopi were waging a wrestling

match. Out of the mound rose a long, glossy stalk, like a neck, and atop this sat a single greenish eye.

It was the Lufless Monster.

All at once the tentacles thrust downward, and the beast dove at Ellen like a torpedo. She closed her eyes and waited for the end to come.

19. Absolute Power . . .

When Edgar was absolutely sure that the Irregulars were far from the Pineycone Pocket, he came down from his tree and looked up at Gristly Jefferson suspended in the trees.

"You idiot!" said Edgar. "All we needed was to regroup and form a new plan. You blew it!"

Then Edgar reconsidered. "No, Edgar, let's face it: *You* blew it. You counted on someone else."

"Ouch!" Edgar objected. But then he relented. "But I'm right. Other people only let you down."

"Right. So whom can you trust?"

"Myself." Edgar nodded and turned away from Gristly Jefferson, leaving him hanging unconscious above.

He picked up Gonzalo's big canteen and sniffed

the liquid inside. He was about to pour it out, when he thought of the seeds.

"Ho ho! Now here's an easy way to turn them all at once!" he chortled. "Just drop the seeds in here, which will counter the effects of the zombie juice!"

"It's almost *too* simple," he replied. "It doesn't even give them a fighting chance."

"Since when do you give fighting chances?"

"Good point. By dinnertime, Imogen and the rest will be on my side once again!"

But then a dark expression passed over him.

"Who says they'll actually be on your side?" he asked himself. "They weren't too happy with you the last time they saw you. And then there's Imogen—that bossy tyrant would only try to take over this operation. Who needs her?"

"Who indeed? But then, what? I need a bigger, bolder plan, something worthy of my intellect. Think, Edgar, think!"

Edgar scanned the site quickly. His eyes fell on the unfinished bowls of beans, the tape recorder, and the canteen he was still holding, and an idea flashed in his head. He cracked his knuckles.

"Brilliant as ever, old boy," he said to himself. "I knew you could do it." Removing toenail clippers, glue, and a thimble from his satchel, he set to work.

When the Midway Irregulars returned empty-handed some time later, they found that their cups had been replenished from the canteen, and next to the cups sat the old tape recorder.

A note by the cups read:

Poppets,

Please sample this new flavor of medicine. I think it's the most delicious yet, and will surely cool you off from all that running about.

With great concern for your thirst,

Ormond the Impossible

"Whew, I am a little parched," said Imogen. She, like her friends, knocked back the liquid in a swift gulp. They all shuddered.

"Tastes about the same," said Gonzalo. "Maybe someone stirred it with a loonroot or two, but that's about it."

"Hey, look," said Mab. "There's a note on the tape recorder. 'Press play.'"

Mab obeyed at once, and again Stephanie's voice rattled out through the speaker. Only this time her words were a little different, and her voice sounded muffled and halting.

"Ten-hut, circus scum. I'm here to tell you . . . of your . . . future instructions."

"Goodie!" said Phoebe.

"Does she sound funny to anyone?" asked Imogen. The rest of the Irregulars shushed her as Stephanie's voice went on.

"The boss . . . is . . . now . . . Edgar."

The Midway Irregulars stared blankly at one another.

"I thought Edgar was the enemy," whispered Mab.

"Mob . . . stop . . . thinking . . . he's . . . the enemy," said Stephanie.

"Oh, okay."

Hidden in a fir tree up above them, Edgar chuckled quietly. "Brilliant to recut Stephanie's tape, using her own words against her."

"Aw, it was nothing," he replied sheepishly.

Stephanie's voice continued to stammer through the speaker.

"Remember, soldiers . . . Edgar . . . rules."

"Yes, I do," whispered Edgar.

"We'll remember, Miss Stephanie," said Phoebe.

"If you . . . screw this up . . . you will be . . . the beast's . . . next meal." The tape clicked to a stop.

"Boy, she sure is serious about Edgar being the new boss," said Gonzalo. "We ain't even found the beast yet, and she's already planning to feed us to it!"

"Where *is* Edgar?" asked Imogen.

"I am here!" Edgar jumped down from the tree, landing in the middle of the Midway Irregulars. He bowed. "How's *that* for unexpected?"

"Well, buckle my belt! It's ol' Edgar!" hollered Gonzalo.

"*General* Edgar, please, Gonzalo," said Edgar. "I am the leader now, remember?"

"That's what the tape recorder says," said Imogen. "But where is Stephanie? Why didn't she talk to us herself?"

"She had business in Cougar Falls. As you heard, she left me in charge," said Edgar.

"Yes, we did hear that," said Merrick.

"Excellent. Now, let's get those balm barrels back to the spring!" said Edgar. The Midway Irregulars looked confused. "Come on people, daylight's a-wasting!"

"Uh, General Edgar, sir?" said Gonzalo. "I fairly well busted my hump dragging five barrels up out of a skinny little cave and down this hillside."

"And an excellent job you did, Gonzo," said Edgar. "Now it's time to take them back."

"But . . . but why, General Edgar?" asked Phoebe.

"Our new mission is to ruin Ormond's money-making scheme. He must not get a drop of this balm. So says Edgar the Supreme!"

The Midway Irregulars shrugged, and Edgar rubbed his hands in glee. Insisting that he be referred to as "Supreme One," Edgar led his new subjects in constructing a sleigh from branches and vines and a tarp from his satchel. This was big enough to pull the four remaining barrels at once, and would make quick work of the job.

With the five Irregulars harnessed to it like horses (and Edgar sitting atop the cargo), the procession cut a regal swath up the hill. As they pulled out of the Pineycone Pocket, Edgar looked back and noticed that Gristly Jefferson had come to and was struggling to get out of his bonds. Edgar shook his head.

"You had your chance, woodsman," he said. "Now see how a real master handles a job like this!"

"Oh, Supreme One, you're such a strong leader," sighed Phoebe as she strained to move forward.

"No chatter!" Edgar called back. "You'll need all your energy to get us up this slope. And . . . I now prefer to be called Edgarus Maximus. Yes, that will do!"

He stripped a length of vine from a passing tree trunk and cracked it like a bullwhip.

"Now, *hiyah*!" Edgarus Maximus stood on his sleigh, like a king overlooking his kingdom, as it rose slowly up the mountainside.

20 . . . Disrupts Absolutely

"Now, this is as it should be," said Edgar to himself as the Midway Irregulars pulled him across the mountain.

"Darn tootin'," he replied.

"I can't wait to see Ormond's face when he gets back and realizes I've foiled his little plan." Edgar chuckled, but his expression quickly soured as his thoughts fell on the magician.

Ormond.

For a brief time he had been Edgar's hero. He had promised Edgar a life of magic and mystery as his apprentice, of travel to faraway places—the life Edgar had always thought he was meant to have.

But it had all been a scam, and Edgar had fallen for it. Worse, Ormond had *known* Edgar would believe his lies—he had marked Edgar as a patsy from the very beginning, and Edgar had proved him entirely right. Edgar's face burned at the memory.

"Well, I'm not the same trusting rube I was then," he muttered to himself. "Ormond would understand that if he saw me now. He would see I'm not one to be messed with."

"Why shouldn't he see? He's so close. You can

make him pay," he replied to himself.

"You're right! I *can* make him pay. I *should* make him pay." Edgar paused in his thoughts. "But I should really get rid of this balm—make sure he can't get it. That's most important . . ."

"There's plenty of time for that," he replied. "But what happens when Ormond finds out I've hijacked his zombies? The element of surprise would be lost . . ."

"That's true." Edgar cracked his knuckles. "So, actually, capturing Ormond is the *smartest* move. Ha! Won't Ellen and Nod and Pet all be surprised when they find out I've single-handedly master-minded this whole affair, and apprehended our greatest foe!"

"They sure will be!"

"You say something, Edgarus Maximus?" Imo-gen panted from the front of the line.

"You bet I did," Edgar said. "Halt! Halt halt halt! There's been a change of plans!"

"Another one?" asked Phoebe.

"Gather round, everyone." Edgar leaped down from his perch, picked up a long stick, and cleared the leaves from a patch of ground. He started draw-ing a diagram in the dirt with the stick. "What we need to do right now is set a trap for Ormond."

"Why? I thought the mission was to keep him from getting the balm," said Imogen.

"Edgarus Maximus doesn't need to explain himself!" Edgar snapped. "Trust me. I know what's best."

"Of course you do!" said Phoebe.

"Now, here's what we're going to do." Edgar walked the Irregulars through the plan, using the diagram he'd drawn. When he was finished, he cracked the stick across his palm. "Got it?"

The Midway Irregulars nodded, but still looked confused. Imogen raised her hand.

"Er, Your Excellency, if you want to capture Ormond, why don't we just drop a net on him?"

"Yeah, I'm big enough to hold that scrawny whoziwhatsit," Gonzalo said. "Plus I got my trusty lasso to tie him up good and tight!"

"Fools!" said Edgar. "You see, this is why I'm in charge. Plans such as those are not big enough, not *terrible* enough for the likes of Ormond. He must know it's *me* who has caught him!"

"Oh, okay," said Gonzalo. "You're the boss, Boss."

"Indeed I am. Ormond said he'd be back in the

morning, so we have a lot of work to do. Gonzalo, disassemble the sled—we need the tarp for the giant balloon. Mab and Merrick, you're on sap duty. Get as much of it as you can. Phoebe, you collect the nettleberries, and Imogen, you cut the vines. Everyone got that? All right, break!"

The Midway Irregulars scattered off into the forest to perform their various jobs, while Edgar sat down with his back against a rock and thought over the brilliance of his plan.

It was quite possibly the most perfect idea he'd ever had. When Ormond returned to the forest tomorrow, he would find the Pineycone Pocket empty and a trail of footprints leading right where Edgar wanted him: a clearing by a cluster of boulders down the hill from where Edgar now was. When Ormond reached the spot, the Irregulars would lasso him with their vines and tie him to the boulders, leaving him completely incapacitated and helpless.

That's when the fireworks would really begin. Directly up the mountain from the boulders, Imogen would release the giant sap balloon, which would roll down the hill straight into Ormond and explode all over him, coating him in the sticky goo. Then Edgar would appear above him with the final insult: a bundle of nettleberries, which would adhere nicely to the sapped magician. Ormond's humiliation would be complete.

"It can't fail!" Edgar exclaimed.

Edgar's minions scurried about at their tasks while Edgar paced in circles muttering to himself. Occasionally he would look up and bark an order, but mostly he practiced the contemptuous speech he planned to deliver to Ormond as part of his triumph.

Everything went according to plan—almost. It was nearly dark before Mab and Merrick returned. And they had very little sap.

"We tried, Your Awesomeness!" they cried. "The trees just wouldn't give us any!"

Edgar stroked his chin. "Blast, that's right! Gristly *did* say it wasn't sap season. Well, we need to get it somehow. The plan depends on it!" He strode back and forth, thinking, until his eyes fell upon the barrels full of balm. He snapped his fingers. "That's it! Balm is gluey, even more so than sap. Plus it smells terrible. Ho ho—we'll use that instead."

A warning stirred in Edgar's heart. He tried to put it aside.

"No no, this is even more perfect," he mumbled. "If Ormond ingests any, so what? It's just a life-extending potion. In fact, we should *keep* feeding it to him—what better punishment than an eternity in chains?"

So the Midway Irregulars assembled the tarp into a large balm balloon, emptying into it three of the four barrels, and set it in position on the hill. They secured it with some of the vines, which Imogen would cut when the time was right. They also prepared the vine lassos and the pile of nettleberries Edgar would throw on Ormond. All the activity took most of the night, and the sun was rising again over the forest by the time they'd finished.

Edgar stepped back to admire their handiwork. His smile was as broad as a Heimertz's, and he couldn't help singing:

So long I've waited, my wrath held,
To finally witness my foe felled,
My genius is unparalleled!
As is my resilience.
Revenge is sweet, but I'm quite picky:
I prefer mine served up sticky!
Though 'twill make Ormond quite sick, he
Must concede my brilliance!

Imogen shook her head.

"Are you sure you want to do this?" she asked. Her voice sounded weak. "Something here feels . . . off."

"*I'm* feeling kind of off," said Mab, rubbing her temples.

"Me too," said Phoebe. "Woozyish."

"And I'm starving!" Gonzalo shouted. The rest of the Irregulars nodded.

This snapped Edgar out of his reverie. "But of course you are," he said. "Plus, you need your medicine."

They sat down to a breakfast of tinned ham and a swallow of "medicine," which seemed to return the Irregulars to their chipper selves. Edgar's own stomach was starting to churn in anticipation. Soon he would have Ormond in his grasp and would finally prove whose was the greater mind.

"Okay, places everyone," he called. "Ormond could be here any second, and I want my moment of victory to be—"

Twang!

A rock sailed out of the trees and struck a vine holding the sap balloon, snapping it in two.

"What was that?" cried Edgar, gazing around. The Irregulars did the same, but could see nothing.

Thwack!

Another rock flew out, breaking another vine.

"Stop it, whoever it is!" screeched Edgar. But he was powerless to stop anything. Rock after rock zinged out from the forest, striking and cutting the vines that held back the balm balloon. With each shot the remaining vines strained harder, until finally the last one broke, and the balloon began to roll down the mountain.

"*No!*" Edgar screamed. "No no no no no no no!"

He ran after the balloon, but it was too late. Edgar might have taken comfort that his plan *would* have worked flawlessly, had it not been sabotaged: The balloon picked up speed as it rolled down the hill in the perfect line that Gonzalo had cleared, and it smashed against the rocks below in a wondrous explosion of amber goop, which completely coated the boulders.

Edgar fell to the ground with his head in his hands. "I can't believe this! Who dares foil my plans?" He looked up at the trees. "Show yourself! Is it you, Ormond?"

There was a faint rustle, and the culprit emerged from the trees. But it was not Ormond.

Instead, Ol' Footsie stepped out from the underbrush.

21. Fetch

Ellen waited, eyes closed, for a monstrous mouth to open and swallow her, or jagged jaws to bite her in half, or a tremendous tentacle to wrap around her and squeeze every breath from her body.

Instead, she felt something squishy brush up the side of her body, like a huge dog's tongue.

She opened one eye. It had not been a tongue but, rather, one of the Lufless Monster's long tentacles. But the gesture had not been hurtful or aggressive. It had been almost . . . affectionate.

The creature swam a little ways away, eyeing Ellen expectantly. Every once in a while it would swim in circles around her, but not threateningly. Ellen was again reminded of a dog, frolicking in a park.

"You're not mean at all, are you?" she asked. Pet, who was still attached to her in its own diving helmet, looked askance at Ellen. "No, Pet, I think our Lufless Monster just wants to . . . *play*."

She grabbed the frond of a nearby *Nepenthes* and yanked it off (much to the displeasure of the plant's gullet, which bit at her). She held out the long leaf to the monster, shaking it.

The creature dove for the frond, grabbed the

other end in a tendril, and yanked on it, like a puppy playing tug-of-war. It and Ellen yanked back and forth for a while, until it pulled the frond away from her and swam off joyfully, waving the frond back and forth like a prized toy.

"See?" said Ellen to Pet. "It's like a big aquatic dog. I don't think it's going to hurt us—*oof*!" The creature had swum back and rammed cheerfully into Ellen, sending them both dangerously close to a thick patch of *Nepenthes*.

Though *Nepenthes* bites were poisonous to creatures like Pet, this one swam about with no care for its safety. Ellen wondered about this until she saw the plants lunge at it; its hair was so course and slick that the teeth seeds slid right off, and none was able to penetrate the beast's hide.

The creature noticed Ellen watching it, and it playfully charged her again. The resulting bump sent her spinning.

"Oof! Okay, we're not going to have much luck searching down here if this thing wants to keep playing. Pet, how do you feel about providing a little diversion?" Pet seemed to sigh in its helmet, but nodded its eye. "Thanks, buddy. I think I know what we can do."

She started swimming back up to the surface of the lake, Pet in tow. It took some time, since they were so far down, and she had to negotiate both the *Nepenthes* and the intermittent tackles of the Lufless Monster, who apparently thought they were playing tag. As she swam, Ellen pulled another long, stretchy *Nepenthes* leaf off its vine and carried it with her. Finally the water started to become less dark, and Ellen and Pet popped back up into the cool air.

Ellen made her way to shore, where she found Archibald Tibbits sitting on the rocky shoal in his diving outfit, rocking back and forth, his arms hugged around his knees. When he saw Ellen climbing out of the water, he rocked so far back he fell over.

"You're—you're alive!" he gasped, scrambling up.

"Of course I'm alive," Ellen replied, pulling off her diving helmet. "You didn't think a little sea monster would do me in, did you?"

"So it is real?" Archibald asked, wide-eyed. "There really is a Lufless Monster?"

"I think 'giant seamonkey' is a better description," said Ellen. "But, yes, there is a very rare creature living in the lake, to go along with the very rare *Nepenthes* plants. This adds up to one thing, Archie: There's a very rare substance bubbling up from a spring somewhere at the bottom of that lake, and I need to find it."

"You're going back in?" Archibald's voice trembled. "But Luffie is dangerous!"

"Luffie? First of all, nothing named *Luffie* is dangerous." Ellen laughed. "Those circus kids were just having some fun when they told you those stories."

She walked along the rocky shore to a tall, solid stone that stuck out of the ground just by the water's edge. She pushed against it, but it did not budge. Satisfied with this, she headed up to the edge of the woods and scrounged among the bracken until she found a stolid tree branch, then returned to the beach. She dug a hole next to the large stone and stood the branch vertically in it. Archibald approached and watched her doubtfully.

"What are you doing?"

"Here, make yourself useful and hold this branch upright."

Archibald took hold of the branch as Ellen tied one end of the *Nepenthes* leaf around it, and the other around the rock, forming a large makeshift slingshot. The *Nepenthes* frond was stretchy like seaweed, and Ellen twanged it a few times.

"What is this for?" asked Archibald.

"You'll see. Just hold that branch steady." Ellen now walked back over to Pet, who sat next to its helmet on the beach. "Are you ready, Pet?"

Pet nodded its eyeball, though it did not look particularly pleased about the situation, and crawled back into the diver's helmet. Ellen took it to the edge of the lake and splashed around in the water. Soon, something greenish broke the calm surface; the casual observer might have thought it a bubble, or a fish, or even a reflection, but Ellen and Pet knew better. It was an eye.

"Ready? Ready, Luffie?" Ellen called out. Archibald nearly fainted as the eye rose even farther out of the water, and the creature swam excitedly in circles. "All right, here it comes!"

Ellen ran back to the slingshot and placed Pet, in its diving helmet, in the *Nepenthes* frond.

"Hold 'er steady, Archie!" she shouted, pulling back with all her might, then *snap!* Ellen let loose the strap, and Pet went flying across the lake.

Luffie took off after the ball-shaped helmet. It swam along the surface of the lake, undulating in and out of the water with the grace of a dolphin.

"I don't believe it," said Archibald, gazing after the creature. "It exists. There are stories, but we were always told they were lies made up by strangers. It doesn't make logical sense, but it's real . . ."

Ellen nodded as she pulled her diving outfit back on.

"Logic only gets you so far, Archie. Just because something makes no sense, doesn't mean it's not true."

Archibald Tibbits did not seem comfortable with

this revelation, but he put his dive suit back on anyway.

"So what was the point of the slingshot, anyway?" he asked. "Aren't you worried about your muskrat?"

"Not at all," said Ellen. "It's just a friendly game of *Fetch the Pet*. My brother and I play it all the time."

22. A Spring Is Sprung

Ellen reasoned that the spring would most likely be located in the thickest crop of *Nepenthes* plants. Archibald dutifully swam behind her, constantly on the lookout for Luffie, whom he still didn't quite trust not to drown him.

Far, far down they reached the bottom of the lake. Even though she adjusted her gauges, the pressure pounded in Ellen's ears, and it was bitterly cold. She tried to put all of this out of her mind as she headed toward the center of the lake, where the *Nepenthes* seemed to grow more densely. Soon they were swimming through a forest of them, and it became quite difficult to avoid the snapping heads.

But as the flora thickened, Ellen noticed something else: Though they were fifty feet down, the water seemed to be *lighter.* Ellen no longer needed the flashlight to see where she was going.

"Archie, are you seeing this?"

"I'm seeing, and that's an improvement."

"It's coming from the plants!" Ellen exclaimed. "The *Nepenthes* are *glowing*!"

And so they were. Soon Ellen and Archibald found themselves in a jungle of bioluminescent shoots.

"I've never seen *Nepenthes* do this before," said Ellen. "We must be getting close."

She swam around a thicket of plants, not even troubling to avoid the biting jaws, and there it was. In the light emitted from the *Nepenthes*, Ellen could see a hole in the ground, and a glowing greenish substance burbling up from it.

"Balm," she whispered, her eyes wide. Archie looked at her and shuddered. In the pale and ghastly green light reflecting off her ashen skin, she looked almost possessed.

"What—what are those?" he asked, pointing at thousands of tiny arrowheads floating just above the lakebed.

"It's another thing that defies logic," said Ellen. "I think your head might explode if you knew."

Ellen reached out and grasped one: a *Nepenthes* seed. She held it out to Archibald.

"These are the plants' seeds. They fall out every night and are replaced with new ones every morning. In the lake they have no place to go, so they must just float—" She stopped abruptly.

"What's wrong?" asked Archibald.

Ellen fingered the seed thoughtfully.

"Archie, where does the town of Lach Lufless get its drinking water?"

"From the lake, of course. I told you it was freshwater."

"Of course!" cried Ellen. "Your town drinks this water, which is full of *Nepenthes* and their seeds. Your disgusting luflins are made from *Nepenthes*. I can't believe I was so stupid!"

"Is the pressure too much, Ellen? Are you losing your mind?"

"No. Listen, you're going to have to take a lot of what I say on faith. So, this green stuff is called balm, and among other things, it can keep a person alive indefinitely, it is extremely flammable, and, in small doses, like what might seep into a water supply, it can make a population overly sweet, happy, and celebratory."

"We should really go before the last of your sanity leaves you . . ."

"Truth without logic, remember? Now, I know you have no basis for comparison, but take it from me, Lach Lufless is unconventionally . . . serious. Your town is nothing like the other towns I've been to that exist near these balm springs, but I know why."

"Yes, I'm sure you do, but—"

"It's the *Nepenthes*!" Ellen exclaimed. "You see, these plants have the exact opposite effect of the balm. I know because I was brought back from a very scary happy place once by the use of these seeds. This lake *is* your water supply, but the expanse of *Nepenthes* overpowers the balm—you even eat the stuff. That's why you all are so sour and dour! What do you think about that, Archie? Archie? *Oof!*"

Something bowled into Ellen, again sending her spinning into the mouths of the chewing plants.

23. That Giant Sucking Sound

Ellen pulled herself from the grips of the tiny mouths—even through the thick suit, she could tell these seeds were particularly sharp.

"Luffie, we really need to teach you to heel," she grumbled as she swam free. Then she felt something seize her and draw her arms and legs together with a force far stronger than any *Nepenthes.*

Ellen's helmet had swiveled around on impact, and she couldn't see a thing. She thrashed wildly about, but whatever held her only grew tighter. She wiggled until her helmet moved back into position, and she could see mesh pressed against the faceplate. She was trapped in a net. But whose?

The answer was quick to come as the face of a once-trusted friend drew close. It was Nod himself.

He was dressed in the high-tech scuba gear she and Pet had found in Stephanie's boat, and for a 200-year-old man, he was an impressively spry swimmer. He adjusted a knob on his helmet, attuning his own radio to the frequency Ellen and Archie were using. Ellen heard his voice crackle in her ears.

"Ah, Ellen, I was hoping you'd scampered back to a nice life in Nod's Limbs instead of pursuing this folly. Alas! Now you shall die a horrible death! But isn't the foliage wonderful down here?"

"Indeed, is most splendid." Madame Dahlia floated up, holding Archibald in another net. Ellen thought she could see tears in the woman's eyes. Was it possible the hypnosis was wearing off, that she was regretting doing what she was about to do?

"The beauty of this garden is seen not even in the stars," Madame Dahlia said, sniffling.

No, apparently the hypnosis was holding just fine.

"Ellen, who are these people? Why have they put us in nets?" Archibald eyed Nod and Madame Dahlia. "If Officer Flemm were here, the two of you would be ticketed for Impolite Use of Fishing Implements. It is unlawful and decidedly rude."

"That's right," said Ellen. "You all wouldn't want to disobey the *law*, would you?"

"Oh, Ellen, haven't you figured it out yet? I'm the law now." Stephanie Knightleigh swam into view and came face-to-face with Ellen. She waved her hand in front of her helmet. "Ugh, I can smell your stench even through the pressurized oxygen."

"Letting your lackeys do the tough work for you again, I see," said Ellen.

"Isn't that the point of lackeys?" Stephanie retorted. "Made all the better since they're like your adopted parents, and don't even get me started on the creepiness of *that*."

Stephanie unhooked a vacuumlike device that was strapped to her back. She placed the end of the hose at the spring opening and flipped a switch. Her machine hummed, and the balm started to disappear up the hose and into a large drum.

Ellen struggled furiously in her bonds, but Nod

held her with unbelievable strength. It was either that, or Ellen was suddenly weakening. Her limbs started to tingle, and it was becoming increasingly harder to breathe.

"The oxygen," she whispered, glancing at her gauge. Her tank was almost empty. She looked at Archibald, who seemed to be feeling the same effects. If they stayed down here much longer, they would both suffocate.

"Stephanie, you have to let us go," she said.

The pump hummed and clumped, hummed and clumped, every second sucking up more and more of the precious substance.

"Talk about déjà vu," said Stephanie. "Let's see if I remember how this goes. You beg for your life, I say I don't care and leave you for dead."

"You forgot the part where I escape."

"And then we'll do this whole thing again in some other time-forgotten place that doesn't offer a decent shower. Really, Ellen, aren't you tired of playing this game? Just accept that I will always get the better of you. A Knightleigh always wins." The pump chugged to a stop; the canister was full. "Oh, look, right on schedule." She turned to Nod and Madame Dahlia. "Leave them for dead."

24. Seeding Victory

Stephanie swam off beyond the glow of the *Nepenthes*.

"It's a shame, Ellen, a real shame," said Nod as he began to tie Ellen's net to a *Nepenthes* stalk. "I always liked you and what's-his-name, almost like you were my own children. Or my own great-great-great-great-great-great grandchildren, as it were. Oh, well, can't be helped!"

Ellen knew better than to waste her breath—and in this case, literally waste her breath—arguing with Nod. Her encounters with those hypnotized by Pilosoculus tears had taught her that they would obey without question the orders their master had given them, no matter how unethical, immoral, illogical, or just plain dumb those orders were. Archibald Tibbits, however, knew no such thing.

"Please, ma'am, this is most . . . inappropriate," he gasped. "This is . . . murder . . . very illegal in these parts . . ."

Ellen had one last idea. Though her legs were cinched tight (and getting tighter) she *could* wiggle her feet. And she wore more on her feet than just footie pajamas.

Clap. Clap. Clap. The muffled sound carried across the water.

"What's that racket?" asked Nod.

"Is Ellen's flippers," said Madame Dahlia. "Flapping as if clapping."

"Must be involuntary muscle response," said Nod, shaking his head. Then something ran straight into him, launching him away from Ellen.

"Luffie!" said Ellen. "Here, tug-of-war!" She held out the net, and like before, Luffie grabbed at it with a tentacle and pulled, quickly wresting away the knots Nod had tied. Pet, in its diving helmet, tucked safely under another tentacle, gave Ellen a weary tendrils-up.

Madame Dahlia dove at Luffie, but the creature thought she was playing. It wrapped its tentacles around her, then spun her like a top. Nod reached out to grab Ellen, who was now free of her net, but again Luffie thought it was a game, one that might have been called Throw the Nod Up and Smack It Around. Soon the water was a swirl of arms and tentacles and plant stalks.

"Dratted animal!" cried Nod as Luffie spun him about. "Always disrupting our work with your infernal play!"

Ellen helped Archibald with his bonds. His eyes were starting to roll up in their sockets, and he was deathly pale.

"Swim up, I'll be right behind you," she said, pulling the last of the net away from him. He nodded vaguely and struggled to kick himself upward, half swimming, half floating toward the surface. When Ellen was satisfied he could make it, she turned back to the scuffling trio.

Her air was preciously low, but Ellen knew it had to last her just a little longer. She swiped at the water and gathered up a handful of the floating *Nepenthes* seeds, then swam into the middle of the melee.

Madame Dahlia was closest. Ellen reached over and yanked her helmet away. The surprised woman gulped in water, but that wasn't all she gulped—

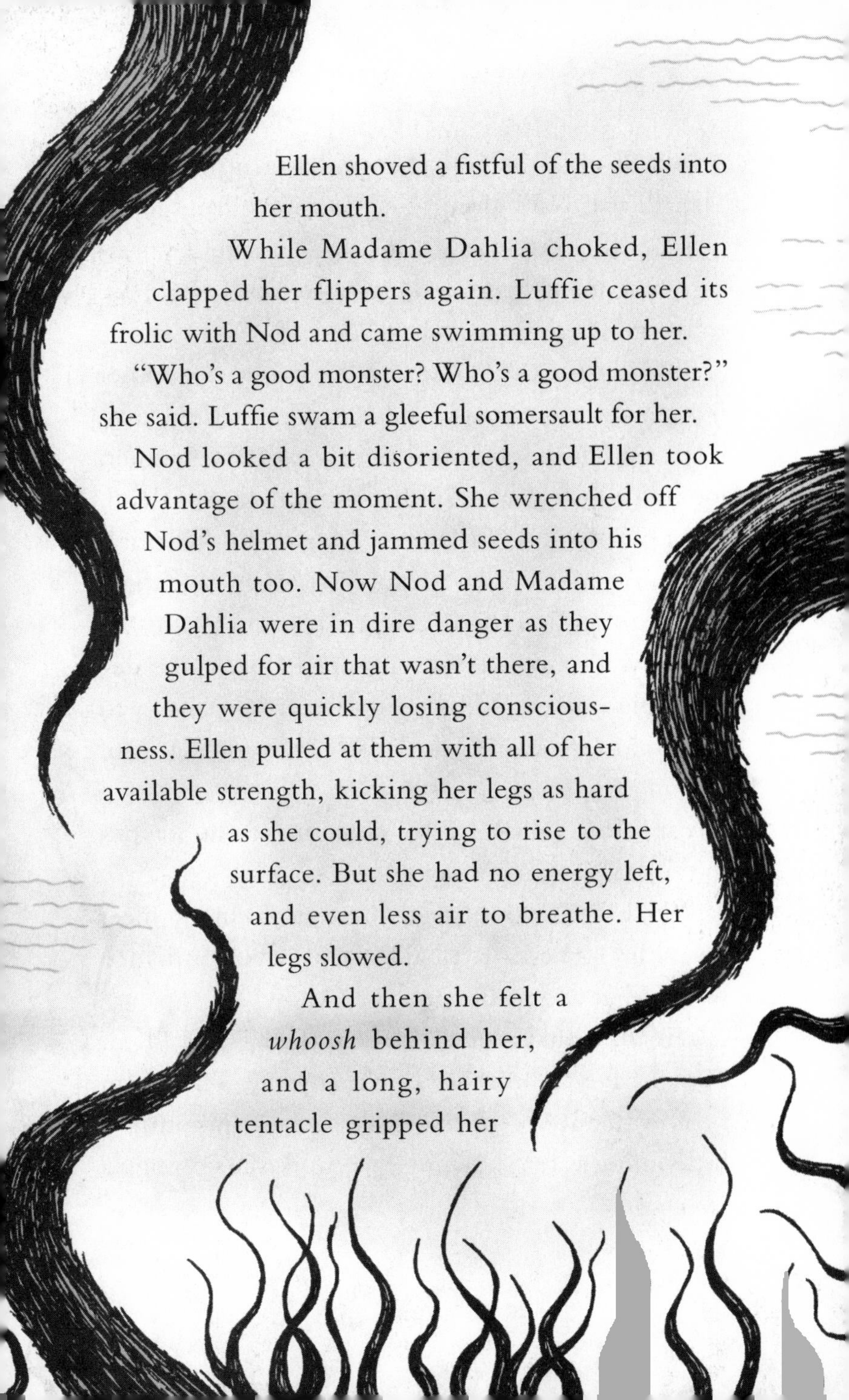

Ellen shoved a fistful of the seeds into her mouth.

While Madame Dahlia choked, Ellen clapped her flippers again. Luffie ceased its frolic with Nod and came swimming up to her.

"Who's a good monster? Who's a good monster?" she said. Luffie swam a gleeful somersault for her.

Nod looked a bit disoriented, and Ellen took advantage of the moment. She wrenched off Nod's helmet and jammed seeds into his mouth too. Now Nod and Madame Dahlia were in dire danger as they gulped for air that wasn't there, and they were quickly losing consciousness. Ellen pulled at them with all of her available strength, kicking her legs as hard as she could, trying to rise to the surface. But she had no energy left, and even less air to breathe. Her legs slowed.

And then she felt a *whoosh* behind her, and a long, hairy tentacle gripped her wrist. She felt herself rising, dragging Madame Dahlia and Nod along with her, up through the heads of the *Nepenthes aquatis*, up to where the pressure was not so great and the water not so cold, up to the gray light of sky above.

Ellen broke the surface of the water, ripped her helmet from her head, and breathed in the clean, fresh air. Pet bobbed to the surface in its helmet, looking a little seasick. Luffie swam the lot of them, including Nod and Madame Dahlia, to the shore, where Archibald was waiting. Together, Ellen and Archibald pulled their former adversaries onto the rocks. With a couple of slaps on the back, the dezombified divers coughed up water and began to breathe more easily, though they were far from dancing a jig.

Far across the lake, Ellen could make out Stephanie's boat, speeding away.

"So that was your friend you were trying to meet up with?" asked Archibald. "You have confirmed my feelings about strangers, you know."

"Yeah, I can't argue with you there," said Ellen. "But I have to hunt her down anyway. That balm I told you about—the stuff she sucked up with her little underwater vacuum—we think she's going to

combine it with other materials and create something horrible. It's up to me to stop her."

"Stop," rasped Nod. He lurched up from the rocks and grabbed her ankle.

"Oh, not *still* a zombie," sighed Ellen. "I've got more seeds I can shove down your throat, old man—"

But Nod's expression softened. "I . . . just wanted to say . . . I owe you . . . enormous-time."

Ellen smiled. "I think you mean *big*-time, Augie."

"As you say." Nod coughed. "Now . . . go stop that shrew."

"My pleasure." Ellen jumped off the stone and ran back into the water, leaving Pet to cradle Nod's and Madame Dahlia's head in its tendrils.

Archibald shook his head and followed her into the water.

"We can't swim that far or that fast," he said.

"We don't have to." Ellen gave a sharp whistle and called, "Heeere, Luffie!"

The Lufless Monster came shooting up through the water, gleeful it still had someone to play with. It nearly swamped Ellen in its enthusiasm.

"Down. Down, I say! Want to play a game of chase, Luffie?" The creature slapped the water with all its tentacles. "Good, good. Okay, we're going to follow that bad, bad girl—and you're going to carry me. Doesn't that sound like fun?"

Luffie extended two tendrils, which Ellen seized like reins. She pulled herself up astride the bulk of its body, as if she were riding a horse.

"Oh, heavens," sighed Archibald. "There is an only-one-child-per-bicycle law in Lach Lufless, but I suppose this creature scarcely counts."

He hauled himself up behind her, and she gave

the tentacle reins a brisk shake. With that, Luffie was off, speeding quickly after the disappearing boat.

25. Kingdom Come

Luffie glided effortlessly across the surface of the lake, all of its tentacles swishing in unison to propel them forward like a missile.

"I—I feel like a mighty porpoise!" called Archibald with uncommon gusto in his voice.

"Think *shark*, Archie," said Ellen. "Or maybe barracuda. Porpoises don't inspire fear in their enemies!"

"Righto!" he said, but the look on his face showed more elation than menace.

It seemed they were gaining on Stephanie. The girl turned and saw her pursuers, but only gave them a carefree wave. Then she casually resumed her driving toward—well, nothing. A shroud of fog obscured the horizon.

"Where is she going?" asked Ellen. "What's on the other side of this lake?"

"We're headed toward Angus MacLuff's dam. Nothing over there but a big wall of boulders," said Archibald.

"You're kidding. She can't escape?"

"Not with her boat. The dam is quite high. Her boat will founder on the stones if she keeps going much farther."

Ellen allowed herself to laugh. "She's speeding into a trap! A Knightleigh *never* wins!"

Stephanie must have realized that she was approaching rocky waters because her boat slowed, though it held course, and Luffie continued to gain. In a moment Ellen could see the long black outline of the unevenly stacked boulders that made up MacLuff's dam. The stones were monoliths—no telling how Angus MacLuff had lugged them around. It was as if a thousand Stonehenges had rained from the sky. Stephanie pulled her boat up to the wall, disembarked, and scaled the rocks one by one. With her canister of balm and a bulky backpack of gear, her going was slow. It was the only hope Ellen had of catching her.

"Looks like she's going to run for it," said Archibald.

"But where? What's on the other side of the dam?"

"Bogs," said Archibald. "Some ponds. A marsh or two. Oh, there's quite a nice moor as well."

"Sounds moist. So where does she think she's going?"

Stephanie crested the top of the dam as Luffie drew up to the base. Ellen scrambled up the moss-covered boulders, and Archibald slid and stumbled along behind his more nimble-footed partner. They often had to jump over gaps in the tumbled stones, and on one particularly slick rock, the small boy slipped and found himself wedged between two boulders.

Ellen turned back to the struggling Archibald.

"Please feel free to continue your chase," he grunted. "I'll, ah, catch up, I'm sure."

Ellen groaned but came back to haul Archibald up to safety. "You're my chaperone, remember?" she said. "Besides, I don't want your broken body on my conscience. Now hurry!"

As they clambered up the wall, they could see drops of green ooze, which soon grew into a thick trail.

"Her balm canister is leaking!" said Ellen. "Boy, did she screw up this plan, or what? It's almost sad."

Finally Ellen made it to the top of the dam and peered over the other side. The fog had lifted somewhat, and she could see the low country beyond. As

Archibald had said, it was a series of gray pools and muddy bogs as far as she could see.

On this side of the dam, the boulders gave way to a thick carpet of coarse grass and bracken, descending steeply fifty or sixty feet to a small lake at the dam's base. Following the green slime trail with her eyes, Ellen saw that Stephanie was drawing close to another boat moored in this tiny lake. This speedboat—slightly bigger than the last—held many more canisters like the one Stephanie was carrying.

"There's no outlet," wheezed Archibald, cresting the dam at last. "These are all shallow ponds connected by only the smallest trickles of water. She's trapped."

"Ha! You might as well be sailing in a bathtub!" Ellen shouted out. Stephanie turned with a smug smile, and Ellen noticed a flare gun in her hand. Stephanie leaped aboard the speedboat and aimed the flare gun at the base of the dam.

"What an oddly unthreatening gesture," said Archibald.

Stephanie fired the gun, and a ball of purple flame burst from the end. The flare burst against the rock—and indeed for a moment it had seemed as odd and unthreatening as Archibald said. But then a column of fire billowed up: The trail of leaked balm had ignited. The force of a small explosion shook the dam under their feet. Another fiery blast followed higher up the dam, and another.

"Archie, balm goes *kerblooey* in fire," said Ellen. "Those drops of balm are going to—yikes!—keep detonating all the way up the slope!"

Pebbles and clumps of mud rained down on them as the series of explosions picked up pace.

Boom! Blam! Blattablattablat!

A plume of fire raced toward them like a burning fuse.

"Over here," cried Ellen. She and Archibald ran along the top of the dam, away from the trail of balm drops they had been following. "We can outrun the explosions, but we have to—oh no!"

Archibald looked where Ellen pointed. An open canister of green balm had been buried in the bracken not ten feet down the slope. But not just one—as they ran they could see that Stephanie had buried a whole series of balm-filled canisters every few feet. From left to right, she had created a line of bombs that would open the dam like a zipper.

"Faster! Faster!" cried Ellen.

They could feel heat flashing against their skin, and

the throbbing sound of exploding balm beat a rhythm in their ears as it drew nearer and nearer. Ellen was sprinting now. She could tell Archibald was falling behind, and she grabbed his wrist to drag him faster.

When the first canister blew, Ellen found she was no longer running forward but *sailing*—in the air, like the shattered rock flying around her. Her feet had hardly touched the ground when the next canister went up, and she tumbled. Ellen and Archibald plunked, flopped, and skidded headlong across the grass. When their bodies stopped rolling, chunks of rock and dirt covered them up until nothing could be seen of them but a striped sleeve and a muddy loafer.

26. Edgar Feels the Squeeze

Massive indeed were the creature's feet. Fully three times as large as a grown man's, they were covered in coarse hair matted with mud and leaves. But above the feet rose—well, another Pet.

It was not like Gristly Jefferson's description.

It was not even like Yehti, the snow monster.

It was so much . . . less.

Ol' Footsie was a diminutive hairball almost identical to the one-eyed creature Edgar had grown up with—aside from its huge feet, of course. The beast's eyelid was squinty with anger, and it wagged a single tendril at Edgar as if to say, "*Naughty, naughty, naughty.*"

"Footsie?" Edgar was incredulous. "You're—you're so . . . *small* . . . and . . . *annoying* . . . Do you know what you've just done?"

The hairy creature bristled and its eye narrowed even further. Edgar returned the glare.

"So that's how it's going to be, is it? I've wrangled with your kind before, you nasty little wig. When I'm through with you—"

Edgar was cut short by Footsie's feet, which had landed squarely on his head. The so-called Squatch battered the boy's skull with a barrage of foot slaps, then leaped away into the forest.

"After it!" cried Edgar. "Catch it! Punish it!"

But before anyone could make a move, another figure appeared from the trees. This one, however, was decidedly human, and it pulled Edgar into a great bear hug.

"Heimertz!" Edgar cried, for indeed, that's who it was: Ronan Heimertz, the twins' groundskeeper. He wore his usual uniform of overalls and a giant smile, and squeezed Edgar so tightly the boy thought his lungs might burst. "Heimertz! Am I glad to see you! Quickly, Ormond will be here any second, and we need a plan B to capture him—hey, Heimertz, that's a little too tight—*gasp* . . ."

Edgar couldn't breathe, and Heimertz would not let go. Edgar could only stare at him with bulging, questioning eyes, and those questions were answered soon enough when Ormond himself emerged from the woods. He laughed heartily at what he saw.

"Oh, Edgar, Edgar, you still do make me chuckle!" Ormond wiped tears from his eyes. "Let up a little, Ronan, won't you? We don't want him dead yet." Ronan relaxed his grip slightly, and Edgar gulped in air.

"Heimertz," he gasped. "Not you . . ."

"I'm afraid so," said Ormond. "*Your* caretaker is

now *my* henchman. This is the end of the road for you, my old apprentice."

"No! I l-lead an army—oog—of my own, now," groaned Edgar. "Irreg—"

Ormond cut Edgar off by shoving a pinecone into his mouth.

"My little Irregulars, why are you not following Stephanie's orders?" asked Ormond.

"Stephanie told us on the tape to follow Edgar," said Imogen. "Sure, she sounded kind of funny, but she *did* transfer authority to him."

"This tape?" Ormond held up the tape player they had left in the Pineycone Pocket. "You believed this? Edgar reedited it, you imbeciles!"

Gonzalo scratched his neck. "A dirty trick, no question," he said. "Still, we did get our orders. Follow Edgar. We kind of, uh, have to obey."

The magician tented his fingers as he thought for a long moment. Then he spoke carefully.

"Children, Stephanie anticipated someone would steal you away from her, so she sent Ronan here with special orders to find your new leader and crush him. So tell Ronan, my poppets: Who is your leader?"

Each of the Irregulars pointed at Edgar.

Edgar's eyes bulged, and he finally found the strength to spit out the pinecone. Had he had proper blood flow to the brain, he might have had wits enough to avoid what he did next.

"It's Ormond . . . *he's* the leader!" Edgar shouted. "It's not me. It's not me! Get him, Ronan!"

"Me?" Ormond asked, shocked. "I am the leader?"

"Y-yes!" Edgar squirmed in the caretaker's grip.

"Got that, children?" asked Ormond.

"Got it," said Imogen. "Ormond's the leader. Not Edgar."

"Wait—wait—oh, cripes!" Edgar gasped. "You were lying . . . Ronan's not . . . under special orders . . ."

"Of course not," said Ormond. "Thank you for transferring your authority to me, you poor deluded dupe."

"I . . . I . . . oh," Edgar whispered.

"Excellent. Now, we'll need to get those barrels back." For the first time, Ormond noticed the three empty barrels and the sap explosion down the hill. "Great gadflies, Edgar, what have you been playing at? Gonzalo, you carry the full barrel. The rest of you, roll the empties on down." The Midway

Irregulars obeyed their new chief without question, and disappeared into the forest with their loads. Ormond also turned to go.

"Oh, and I think I'll just take this for safekeeping." He picked up Edgar's satchel and slung it over his arm.

"You fiend! It n-never did anything t-to you—"

"Well, *you* won't be needing it anymore." He nodded at Heimertz and followed after the Irregulars. "Finish him, Ronan."

"Hei-Heimertz . . . don't . . . do this," grunted Edgar as two massive hands pressed him like a trash compactor, and he felt the last of the air whoosh out of his lungs. The giant man stood motionless, grinning as he ever grinned, silent as he was ever silent. Still his hands squeezed harder and harder. Before he had become their ally, Heimertz had been the only thing Edgar and Ellen had ever truly feared. Now Edgar realized the full danger of being his enemy.

Edgar felt himself growing faint—but he was determined that if Heimertz were going to kill him, he would meet the man's gaze, eye to eye, until his last moments.

Thus Edgar saw the aspen log just before it crashed down on Ronan Heimertz's head.

Edgar fell to the ground, gasping for air. When he looked up he saw Gristly Jefferson standing above him, feet planted apart, fists out like a boxer. Heimertz lay on the ground, dazed but not completely unconscious.

Gristly grabbed Edgar and pulled him off into the woods.

"You . . . got free . . ." Edgar began.

"When I woke up this morning, I was safely on the ground, ropes untied. And there were two big footprints right next to my head. I figure Footsie knew you needed help."

They could now hear rustling behind them: Heimertz had risen and was crashing through the woods after them. They quickened their pace.

"I'm sorry I left you tied up back there," huffed Edgar as he ran. "I really botched this operation."

"I'm not about to disagree."

Heimertz's pounding feet sounded like a charging rhinoceros, and he gained on them with every step.

"Tuck and roll, Sally, tuck and roll!" chuffed Gristly Jefferson.

The woodsman jammed an elbow into Edgar's ribs and sent the boy sprawling left just as he dove right. At that moment, Heimertz charged between, straight into a thick bush.

Swoop!

One of Edgar's modified net traps sprang. The trigger cable worked perfectly, just as Edgar had intended, and the boom arms swept upward on cue to draw the net around their prey. Now Ronan Heimertz swung like a side of beef.

"Nice modifications," said Gristly.

"Nice maneuvering," said Edgar. "You were *trying* to get him to chase you, weren't you?"

Gristly Jefferson winked. "This should hold him until—"

A sound like a groaning tree came from the trap. Heimertz had gripped the net and was straining to rip the rope in two.

"Heimertz!" called Edgar. "It's me, Edgar! You don't have to fight me. Fight the hypnosis, instead. Resist it!"

For a moment Heimertz let go of the trap, and Edgar thought he saw the man shudder. An unearthly whisper clawed its way out of Heimertz's throat.

"*Run.*"

Then he gripped the rope with renewed strength, and the rope began to tear apart.

"Do as he says!" said Gristly. "Find a way to fix this, Sally. *Fast.* I'll hold this guy as long as I can!"

Edgar turned on his footie and charged into the forest. He had no idea what to do next.

27. Aftermath

Grit filled Ellen's eyes, her mouth, her nostrils. She pulled herself from the rubble, and for a moment thought she had gone blind. Then she felt a cool, wet breeze blowing and saw that thick clouds of dust were just beginning to clear from the eruption. Archibald poked his head out of the dirt, choking and hacking.

Angus MacLuff's massive dam had been completely blown apart. The water of the great Lach Lufless lake now rushed down into the low country, overfilling the smaller lakes beneath them. The rising waters spilled over their banks, linking the smaller lakes and forming channels between them. Ellen watched with a sickening pang in her stomach as the great lake drained into the land below. And amid the crashing river, Ellen spied a lone green stalk with a single eyeball atop rushing along.

"Luffie!" she cried.

The creature looked at her with confusion and alarm growing in its eye. The current held the Lufless Monster in its grip, sweeping it over the busted dam and away downstream.

There was nothing they could do for it but watch as it rode the floodwater. In a moment Luffie's craned neck was indistinguishable from the shattered branches and limbs and other debris littering the incessant stream.

"Hang tough, Luffie!" Ellen called. "You'll wash up in a comfy lagoon somewhere, you'll see!" In a smaller voice, she asked Archibald: "Right?"

"I do hope so," he said. "Surely, it's more likely than your friend surviving this madness, yes?"

"No such luck," said Ellen. "Look!"

Floating along the torrent was Stephanie's boat. Stephanie turned and waved at Ellen as the cresting tide carried her farther and farther away over what had once been shallow ponds and marshes.

"We have to go after her!" cried Ellen, yanking Archibald up off the ground. "She's getting away! Quick, we need a boat, a plane—anything. Aha! Here comes our chariot!"

Ellen pointed at a tilting pontoon boat that was

chugging toward them from Lach Lufless. It had a siren blaring, and Officer Flemm stood at the front, surrounded by several other lawmen. When Officer Flemm noticed he was speeding toward a broken dam, he veered wildly to the side, trying to reach the safety of the shoreline. Ellen waved her arms wildly at him and he steered toward her, the motor of the boat straining to resist the pull of the waterfall.

"Archie, we need to commandeer that boat and ride it down the current," said Ellen. "You make a distraction, and I'll—*achoo!*"

Ellen let loose a violent sneeze. She wiped her mouth with her sleeve and blotted her watery eyes.

"Whoa. That's a lot of dust. Anyway—"

But before she could finish her sentence, Archibald had whipped out a notepad. He handed Ellen a slip of paper.

"What!" Ellen stared openmouthed at her third ticket. "Archie—why—what did I do now?"

"You sneezed without covering your mouth," said Archibald. "Such things contribute to the spreading of germs and general air pollution."

"*Air pollution?* Stephanie just *blew up the dam*! All this dirt in the air? She caused it!"

"And she will be getting her ticket," said Archibald. "But it will still only be her first."

By now Officer Flemm and his crew had climbed to the top of the dam.

"Sirs, we have a third-timer up here," said Archibald. Ellen started to flee, but Archibald tripped her, and she landed right at the feet of Officer Flemm. He grabbed her arm tight and hauled her up.

"But Stephanie Knightleigh is getting away!" she screamed, struggling wildly. "How can you arrest me when she could have killed someone?"

But no one answered what Ellen thought was a perfectly logical question. As she was dragged to the horrible punishment that awaited her in Lach Lufless, her shrieks faded away into the dusty air:

Let go of me! You've got it wrong—
I've been your ally all along!
Ouch! You coppers sure are strong,
You lumbering, oafish apes.
Archie, curse your stickler's spite!
And—hey, lay off the braids, all right?
Let me point out your oversight:
The real villain escapes!

28. Sticky Stock

When the sun rose the next morning, or, rather, when the sky turned from black to a lighter slate color, Ellen was brought to the public pillory in Town Square. There stood a set of stocks she was to be chained in.

Only this was not the usual wooden stockade such as was used in olden times. This one was solid but sticky, and it smelled of Popsicles. But other than that, it was a proper stockade, with Ellen's head and arms locked in holes so that she was forced to hunch over.

Archibald Tibbits appeared out of the shadows.

"Archie, you weasel," Ellen growled.

"Careful—comparing people to animals is a tick-etable offense," he said. "Then again, perhaps you said *measles*."

"I thought we were on the same side."

"I'm not on any side, Ellen. You broke the law. The law is everything in our town."

Ellen sighed. "And you just let Stephanie sail off into the sunset, off to her happy ending."

"She will not be welcomed back."

"I'm sure she's really bent out of shape about that."

"I think you are speaking with sarcasm," said Archibald. "I find that you do that frequently."

"I know it's like a foreign language to you, Archie," said Ellen. "But you should try it sometime. Expand your horizons." She shifted uncomfortably in her stockade and found that her pigtails had stuck to it, pulling at her scalp. "What the heck is this made of?"

"Rock candy," said Archibald.

"You've got to be kidding me," said Ellen "Why on earth do you lock people in candy? *This* is the terrible punishment for getting three tickets?"

"In addition to the abject shame you will face when people walk by and stare at you, the only way to escape is to lick yourself out of the horrid bonds of sweetness."

"You mean if I can lick my way out, I'm free?"

"Yes, and I am sorry for your fate. You will have an awful bellyache when you are through. And by this time next month, you will find your teeth rife with cavities. What a horrible thing to face."

"Yes, how will I go on?" said Ellen.

A *putt-putt-putt* sounded in the distance, and Ellen smiled when she saw a familiar blot in the sky. It flew closer and closer, until it was almost above

them. Archibald looked up in time to see a rope drop from the dirigible and lasso the stockade.

"This is my ride," said Ellen. "I'll see you around, Archie."

And then Archibald Tibbits smiled for the first time since he had met Ellen just a day earlier.

"Can't wait," he said, grinning.

The rope pulled taut and Ellen felt herself being reeled into Nod's flying machine through a bomb-bay door in the cabin.

"Why, Ellen, where have *you* been?" asked Nod with a wink.

"Nowhere in particular," said Ellen. "So you two are, uh . . ."

"Thanks to you, my dear, we are both sharp as snacks," said Nod.

"He means tacks, and yes, Ellen, you have freed our minds from such a prison," said Madame Dahlia.

"I'm glad to hear it," said Ellen. "Because while you were zombified, you guys were real jerks."

"I do not understand," said Madame Dahlia, seizing the stockade. "It is candy?"

"Yes, don't ask," said Ellen. "Just get me out of it."

Madame Dahlia cracked the restraints apart, and Ellen stretched out. As she did so, Pet leaped happily into her gut.

"Oog! Okay, okay, good to see you too, hairball."

"No time for mushy reunions," said Nod. "Look at this devastation."

He gestured to the lake, or, rather, to what was left of it. Almost all of the water had drained away, leaving only a muddy crater. The lengthy stalks of the *Nepenthes aquatis*, some eighty feet in length, lay bedraggled along the lakebed, sucking up the last of the moisture available to them. They were dying. Ellen wiped a tear from her eye.

"It's not fair," she said. "Stephanie's destroying everything in her path—even Luffie got swept away downstream. *And she's getting away with it!*"

"Not for long, she isn't," said Nod. "I haven't been dragging my tired old body halfway around the world for my good health. That queenie is going to pay for this."

"Look!" said Madame Dahlia, pointing to the floor of the lake. "It is the spring, or what used to be."

Nod flew lower to the ground. Indeed, they spotted the place where balm had once bubbled up into the water. Now only a small stream of balm seeped out, and it turned to powder almost immediately upon hitting the air. Puffs of it blew away in the chill breeze.

"And now she's destroyed another spring," said Ellen.

"Did you discover where she goes?" asked Madame Dahlia. "Even when we were under her spell, she did not tell us her plans."

"Do the letters *CF* mean anything to you?" said Ellen. "It's all I've got. They were scrawled in Stephanie's hotel room in Frøsthaven. *LL* and *CF*—

well, I found Lach Lufless, and Edgar went in search of whatever *CF* is."

Madame Dahlia glanced at Nod.

"There is place with those letters," she said. "Cougar Falls. It is one of locations where my family travels."

"Then there's a balm spring there!" cried Ellen. "That's where we have to go. That's where we'll find Edgar."

Nod and Madame Dahlia exchanged worried looks.

"What is it?" asked Ellen.

"The Knightleigh witch did tell us some things while we were under," growled Nod. "We know who she's been working with."

"And?" Ellen was practically ready to explode.

"It's Ormond, Ellen." Nod tented his fingers. "Ormond is back. He and Stephanie have been traveling the world, collecting balm with the intent of selling it to the highest bidder."

"This is about money? Not the fate of humanity?"

"Perhaps . . . though some things don't yet add up," said Nod. "The problem at hand, however, is that if Ormond wasn't here with Stephanie . . ."

"He might be in Cougar Falls!" Ellen finished.

"We've got to find Edgar! He's pretty screwy about Ormond as it is. If he's had to face him himself—"

"We will get there in good speed." Nod patted Ellen on the shoulder. "Or my name isn't Augustus Tiberius Nod!"

29. To Fall or Not to Fall

Edgar tried hard to reason as he ran. He needed the seeds of the *Nepenthes arcticus* to save his friends—but, alas, the seeds were in his satchel, and his satchel had fallen into foul hands.

He wracked his brain. The distant sound of Heimertz breaking free from the trap didn't help him concentrate, neither did the sounds of Gristly's frightened shouts. With nothing left to lose, Edgar wandered deeper into the woods, following the one meager idea that occurred to him.

"I know you're out there," he shouted. "I need your help—but I can help you too. Come on out, Footsie."

The forest was silent. Edgar took a few steps toward a stand of scraggly aspen trees.

"I know you don't trust me, but I wasn't the one

who stole your food source!" Edgar called. "Not *technically*, anyway. And I was trying to bring it back . . . sort of."

Nothing stirred. Edgar scowled and scratched his chin. He hopped up on a fallen tree and cupped his hands to his mouth.

"All right, all right. I'll admit that when I had a chance to stop the guy responsible for it all, I blew it. It was a ridiculous snare, and stupider still to use the balm in it—Imogen was right about just throwing a net over him. But I'm sorry, okay? You've got to believe me. I'm sorry, and I can fix this!"

A small tuft of black hair poked out from under a branch. A brown eye blinked as it stepped into the light. And step it did, on two ridiculous feet.

"I can stop them, Footsie. I can stop this whole thing. But I need to know where the spring is."

Edgar immediately regretted his words. The creature's eyeball turned savage and it zipped into the shadow of the fir like a hermit crab into its shell.

"I didn't mean it like that!" cried Edgar desperately. "The plants! The *Nepenthes*! Those little snapper shoots, that's what I'm after! Please . . .

the . . . the fate of humanity hangs in the balance."

Edgar plowed through the trees, parting branches to look for the Squatch. But if the creature didn't want to be found, Edgar knew it wouldn't be.

He plunked down on the ground and hung his head in his hands.

"I've made such a mess of things," he said.

He got up and began to pace.

"But why should everything be up to me?" he demanded. "I'm only a kid, for crying out loud! My life was perfectly fine back in Nod's Limbs. A little dull, sure, but Ellen and I were plenty happy living with Nod and Heimertz and Dahlia and Pet, and then we get pulled into some unbelievable nonsense about saving the planet from a fountain of youth no one understands anyway. I don't even know what I'm doing out here. Why me? What's so special about *me*?"

He shook his fist at the trees, at the squirrels, at the air, at nothing.

The underbrush rustled, and Ol' Footsie emerged. It stared at Edgar with a narrowed eye. Edgar stared back. When he spoke, his words were even and deliberate.

"If you want to lead me to the spring, I will try

to stop what is about to happen. If you don't, well, I understand that too."

The Squatch peered at him, as if trying to decide if this was a boy to be trusted. Finally, it blinked once and headed off into the woods at a quick pace, but not so fast that Edgar could not keep up.

And so Edgar followed the creature through the forest. The Squatch ran quite swiftly on its two clunky feet, and it leaped over streams and logs far more smoothly than Edgar did. Soon Edgar could hear a roaring sound, and it grew louder with every step.

They came upon a precipice so suddenly that Edgar nearly toppled over it. He peeped over the side of the cliff.

He was on a rocky platform halfway down the most enormous waterfall he had ever seen. The crash of the water was deafening, and after so many days in the quiet woods, he thought his ear drums would burst. Spray from the falls pelted him until he was wet through, and the rock on which he and Footsie stood was perilously slippery.

"So this is the actual Cougar Falls?" Edgar shouted over the din. Footsie nodded back at him, then did something that made Edgar's heart plummet harder than the falling water: Footsie jumped.

The creature plunged off the rock and fell with the water into a pool below. It was lost to sight in the churning roil.

Edgar gazed over the edge after the Squatch. His stomach flip-flopped. It was at least a fifty-foot drop, and if that didn't kill him, like as not he'd be drowned by the pummeling falls. But that's where Footsie had gone.

"It's either leading me to the balm spring or to a premature death," Edgar said to himself. "But I must find my courage! As a wise man once said, cowards die a thousand deaths, but the valiant taste of death only—*waughh!*"

And with that, Edgar slipped on some moss and fell end over end off the cliff.

30. In the Grotto

Edgar hit the water so hard, he thought the force would push his organs out of his body. It felt briefly like he had landed on concrete, but a moment later the falls were pushing him under, and he was caught in an undertow, unable to breathe, unable to escape. The water pushed and pulled at Edgar, and he was so dazed, he couldn't even tell which way to try to swim. Had Footsie really meant for him to die?

He felt something grab his wrist, and then he was being dragged through the current. He didn't fight against it. The pounding in his ears stopped, and his head popped up into the air. Edgar, coughing and sputtering, took a few huge breaths. His brain was still addled, but he thought he knew where he was.

He was floating in the part of the pool *behind* the waterfall. Above him the rock jutted out, forming a natural cave, and the water flowed over that, covering the cavern mouth. Edgar was transfixed: It was like a curtain of water, and the wet rock around him shimmered like crystal.

Footsie still had a tendril wrapped around his wrist, and when Edgar had regained his breath, it began to swim again, pulling him with it deeper into the cave. Its two huge feet made for powerful flippers, and it swam steadily and strongly.

The water grew shallower as they neared the back of the grotto, and soon Edgar was able to stand and wade after Footsie. His muscles ached and his bones felt broken, and the air was dark and cool, but still Edgar smiled when he saw the plants growing up out of the shallow pool: *Nepenthes.*

They were much like the ones in Nod's Limbs, except for being slightly hairier and having a swirl of fringe resembling a handlebar moustache above the mouth. He hurried toward them.

"Thanks, Footsie. I promise, you won't regret—*whoa*!"

Footsie gave Edgar a swift kick to the rump, and he tumbled straight into the cluster of plants.

Chomp!

"Ow! Rotten plants! Get off—"

Chomp! Chomp! Chomp!

It was only natural, of course, for the plants to bite him with their seed-lined mouths, but unlike Ellen, Edgar had little appreciation for the wonders of plant life. Cursing and howling, he fumbled out of the *Nepenthes* patch, the plants swarming at him like piranhas.

Making a noise that sounded very much like a chuckle, Ol' Footsie waved once at Edgar with a tendril, then disappeared.

The plants had gotten many good bites at Edgar's bottom, and several seeds were sunk in his flesh. He plucked them out and breathed a sigh of relief.

"Not how I would have chosen to get them," he said. "But I'll take it."

31. Ready, Aim, Fear

Edgar wandered back through the forest, listening for any sign of Ormond and the Midway Irregulars or Gristly and Heimertz, but he heard none.

"Nodspeed, Gristly," Edgar said. "I hope you're a match for Heimertz. I've got to follow the balm."

Edgar found his way back to the place where they had set the trap for Ormond. Fortunately the magician's trail was easy enough to follow: He had had the Irregulars roll the empty barrels of balm down through the woods, and they left wide berths in the leaves.

Edgar tracked them back to the Pineycone Pocket. The Midway Irregulars were seated in a row on the large fallen tree trunk, glumly munching a lunch of beans. It appeared Ormond was giving them a good talking to, and they stared listlessly at their food. At the edge of the clearing, the barrels were gathered, and next to those was Edgar's satchel.

"If only I had my satchel." Edgar shook his head. "All my supplies are in there."

"Then I guess you'll have to improvise." He nodded and glanced over the forest floor until he found inspiration: the hollow stalk of the Gershwin reed.

He yanked it from the ground and returned to the edge of the Pineycone Pocket.

With Ormond there, and Heimertz liable to return any minute, Edgar dared not try to sneak too near. He slunk as close as he could, then shinnied up a tree, using the branches as coverage. From his new perch, he had a direct line of sight to the Midway Irregulars. Ormond paced to and fro with his back to Edgar, and was so consumed in his speech, he didn't notice the slight rustling Edgar's creeping made.

"I just can't believe you all fell for such a juvenile trick," Ormond was saying down below. "The tape was so obviously tampered with."

"Yes, Ormond." The Irregulars hung their heads dejectedly.

Edgar pushed a *Nepenthes* seed into one end of the hollow reed and put the other end to his lips.

"Now, once and for all, who is your master?"

"You are, Ormond."

"And if you see head or footie of either of those infernal twins, what are you to do?"

"Kill them, Ormond."

"That's right. Now, where was I?"

Edgar took aim and blew. The seed shot out of

the reed and—*plop*—landed squarely in Imogen's bowl.

"Bull's-eye!" Edgar whispered. He loaded another seed into his makeshift peashooter.

"We have met with a setback, but all is not lost," Ormond continued. "We have one barrel of the balm, and with some effort, we can fill the rest by morning. And when I say *we,* I mean *you.*"

Plunk. A seed bounced off Gonzalo's chest and into his beans. No one noticed a thing.

"Gonzalo, you will carry the full barrel to town with me," said Ormond. *Plink. Plank.* Seeds shot into Mab's and Merrick's bowls. "The rest of you, stay here with the empty barrels. When Ronan returns, inform him he must get them all refilled."

The Irregulars were nearly finished eating. Imogen had begun to gag slightly, like she had something stuck in her throat, and Gonzalo rubbed his stomach.

Ptooey! The fifth seed shot out of Edgar's peashooter and hit Phoebe's knee.

"Drat," Edgar cursed.

Now Mab and Merrick were starting to react to the seeds they had ingested. Only Phoebe paid rapt attention to Ormond; the others hacked and spat, or just simply stared dazedly off into space.

"What is wrong with you lot?" Ormond demanded. "Thump one another on the backs and be done with it! We have work to do!"

Edgar reloaded and tried again. This time the seed flew straight into Phoebe's bowl just as she was spooning out her last bite.

"All right," Edgar murmured. "Heimertz could be back any time now. It's now or never." Edgar nodded to himself and leaped down from the tree. He strode confidently into the clearing.

"What's this, Ormond? Any old hiker can just waltz into your powwow? I'd expect better security from such a criminal mastermind."

Ormond glared coldly at Edgar. "What can I say? I have but simpletons to work with here. However, they do have their advantages. Irregulars? What do we do when we see a twin?"

"We k-k-k-kill them?" Phoebe asked faintly. She was now also starting to sputter and cough. The others remained silent and looked from Edgar to Ormond and back again.

"Imogen! Gonzalo! Mab! Merrick! Phoebe!" Edgar cried. "You've been poisoned! I've fed you the antidote—you can feel it working. You know

I'm right. Ormond is the enemy! He's enslaved you! He's made you do terrible things!"

"Pish-posh, boy," said Ormond. "They haven't left my sight. So unless you have mastered the art of invisibility and thus snuck into camp and delivered the antidote unseen, which I highly doubt given your meager talents, then—"

Ormond could not finish his sentence, for all five Midway Irregulars tackled him at once.

"That's for betraying your kin!" yelled Imogen, pummeling Ormond in the side.

"That's for making us steal balm!" cried Merrick, pulling at Ormond's hair.

"And that's for turning me into a zombie!" screeched Phoebe, pouring dirt on Ormond's face.

"Children—*oof*—children! This is a misunderstanding!" Ormond pleaded, to no avail.

Gonzalo lifted up the escapist extraordinaire and wrapped him tightly in his lasso; Edgar took great pleasure in tying the knots.

"Escape from that, you faker," he said.

"Edgar, watch out!" cried Phoebe as Edgar felt something hoist him into the air.

Heimertz had returned, and Gristly Jefferson was nowhere to be seen.

"That's right, Ronan. Crush him like the bug he is!" screamed Ormond.

The Midway Irregulars jumped on Heimertz and tried to wrestle Edgar away from him, but it was like watching flies attack a horse: Heimertz just swatted them away. Once again Edgar could feel the life being crushed out of him.

"Heimertz . . . no . . ." he squealed. He exhaled what surely would be his final breath.

Boom!

A purple flare shot up over their heads and exploded in the nighttime sky.

Heimertz dropped Edgar like a moldy cabbage. Without a word the hypnotized man strode out of the Pineycone Pocket.

"What? Stop! I command you!" Ormond howled. He threw his trussed up body in Ronan's path. "You are under orders—*strict orders*—to do as I say."

Heimertz plucked Ormond off the ground and held him up to his face. Dangling from Ronan's grip, Ormond cowered. Ronan heaved two words at him like shot puts:

"*New orders.*"

He tossed Ormond aside as if he were an empty

banana peel, and the magician smacked against a pine and fell to the ground unconscious. Before striding off, Heimertz picked up the last barrel of balm and slung it over his shoulder. Then he was gone.

"What just happened?" cried Imogen.

"It sounds like . . . someone supplied Heimertz . . . with instructions . . . without telling Ormond," Edgar wheezed, still recovering his breath.

"To do what?"

"I don't know . . . but I think . . ." But Edgar could not finish his sentence, for right then stars swam before his eyes, and he passed out cold.

32. Lost and Found and Lost

Ellen scanned the hills of Grayweather Province with a pair of binoculars jammed to her face. The town of Cougar Falls could be seen in the early morning light, but only just barely—a thick, unseasonal haze hung over it all.

"Can't see a blasted thing!" muttered Ellen.

As Ellen whipped her binoculars in all directions, she leaned so far out of the airship's windows that

Madame Dahlia seized her waist in worry.

"Not to be risking such a thing!" cried Madame Dahlia.

"We can't afford to miss Edgar!" said Ellen.

"We'll find him," said Nod from behind the ship's steering wheel. "Or my name isn't Augustus Cornelius Nod!"

"I thought your middle name was Tiberius," said Ellen.

"Oh, I'm just trying a few on for size," said Nod. "How do you feel about Octavius instead?"

"Bah! This is no time for your crazy act, Nod!" fumed Ellen. "We've got serious work to do!"

"It is *always* time for a crazy act!" thundered Nod. "Such as this one!" Nod leaned hard on the steering wheel and pulled back on a steel lever. The blimp went into a steep dive.

"Whoa! What are you doing?" cried Ellen.

"Rescuing Edgar!" he called. "What are *you* doing?"

The sky visible in the windshield was replaced with a vista of the ground. The view spun before them as the dirigible plummeted downward.

Madame Dahlia gave a cry of glee. "Most wonderful man! You have done it! Look, Ellen—"

Ellen looked to where Madame Dahlia was pointing, and sure enough, there, next to a wide, dark crater, they saw a plume of blue-gray smoke and the twinkle of a dying campfire. Through the haze they could see several dark shapes huddled around the flames for warmth. One of them was decked from head to toe in stripes.

"You found him, Octavius!" said Ellen. "Now, uh . . . is it time to pull up?"

Nod winked. He stuck out his jaw as he concentrated on the wheel.

"Pilosoculus!" shouted Nod at Pet. "Blast away!"

Pet, wearing a nautical captain's hat, saluted and pulled the chain. A motor under the floorboards roared, firing torrents of compressed steam from vents around the gondola. To Ellen, thrown against the floor, it felt like brakes being applied in midair. Right before the blimp plowed straight into the hill below, Nod hit the lever again and gave the steering wheel a whirl. The craft leveled out, even as it rotated end for end. Ellen's stomach sank halfway to her footies. But the craft set down at last, and they hadn't died in a fiery explosion.

"I could have thrown in a barrel roll at the end,"

said Nod, "but I didn't feel this was the time for showing off."

"Glad you restrained yourself," said Ellen, peeling herself from the floor.

"Ahoy!" came a voice from below. "Friend or foe?"

"Edgar!" Ellen couldn't wait for the gangplank to be lowered. She leaped out of the gondola and shinnied down the anchor chain that descended to the ground. She saw her brother standing before the fire and ran to throw a loving headlock on him—but she stopped short when she saw he was surrounded by the Midway Irregulars. She looked at them skeptically, and she noticed they were doing the same to her.

"Sister?" Edgar demanded. "Or *zombie*?"

"I should ask you the same thing," she replied.

She bent her knees in a defensive posture, and the others did the same. Seven pairs of fists went up.

"We've got you outnumbered," said Edgar.

"In fists but not brains," said Ellen.

"You're a lumpy-headed nitwit and you stink of seaweed," said Edgar.

"You're a half-brained mouth-breather who drools on himself," said Ellen.

At last they hugged. "I knew you wouldn't get zombified, Brother," said Ellen.

"It was a close call, Sister."

"You'll never believe this," said Ellen. "I almost had Stephanie, but she got away and destroyed the balm spring—"

"Actually, I would believe it," said Edgar. "Wait until you hear this . . ."

33. Zimmizoka

Nod, Madame Dahlia, and Pet joined the group as the Irregulars stoked the fire and whipped up some coffee in a battered camp pot. They inspected the crater at the edge of the campsite. Thin columns of smoke escaped the rubble scattered across the basin.

"This crater was not here last time," Madame Dahlia said.

Nod grunted. "I see now. This haze—it's not fog. It's *dust.* From an explosion."

"An explosion!" said Madame Dahlia. "You don't mean . . . *another* balm spring has gone booming?"

"*Boom* hardly describes it," said Edgar. He and Ellen joined them at the crater's edge.

"Tell me everything, boy, from the beginning," said Nod. "Leave out no detail."

Edgar brought them up to speed on his discovery of the Irregulars, the appearance of Ormond, and the brainwashed villainy of Heimertz.

"Not my Ronan!" cried Madame Dahlia. "He is filled with the strength of five circus bears. This terrible potion cannot hold him long!"

"It held him long enough," said Edgar. "When that purple flare went up, it was like someone flipped a switch. He took the last of the balm and escaped."

"Where? We must follow!" cried Madame Dahlia.

"Hold," said Nod grimly. "Where's Ormond?"

Edgar gave a weak smile and gestured to something suspended in the treetops. It looked like an enormous cocoon made of canvas. "We've got him under wraps."

The Midway Irregulars joined them, and Gonzalo handed Madame Dahlia a fist-size rock. "I know it ain't much, ma'am, but whenever I feel a little low, I just chuck a rock at Ormond up there. Might make you feel better."

"Thank you, dear boy," said Madame Dahlia, touching his cheek. "Not just yet. Soon maybe."

"So when did the balm spring explode?" asked Ellen.

"Just after ol' Ronan flew the coop," said Gonzalo. "We heard a helicopter—well, everyone but Edgar did. He was still laid out as cold as a cast-iron commode. After that whirlybird took off, a whole chunk of the hillside went missing in a big ball of light. Rained dirt and twigs for the better part of twenty minutes. My ears are still ringing from the sound."

"Stealing balm and blowing up balm springs," said Ellen. "Who does that sound like?"

Nod and Madame Dahlia nodded wearily.

"Miss Purple Flare drained a bunch of balm and destroyed the spring in Lach Lufless too," Ellen said. "I'll bet she was the one who fired the signal flare that sent Heimertz running."

Edgar cracked his knuckles. "Including Nod's Limbs that's four balm springs destroyed. All this destruction—just to sell this stuff to the highest bidder?"

"If money is the goal, why would anyone blow up the source of their income?" asked Ellen. "What's that about?"

"*I'll* tell you what it's about." Augustus Nod kicked a pebble into the smoldering crater. "Miss Stephanie Knightleigh has had a secret agenda the whole time she's been collecting balm for Ormond. She gave Ronan special instructions to follow her, instructions not even Ormond knew about. She has something else planned."

Everyone fell silent as the old man paced around the campsite with a mad look in his eye.

"She needed Ormond's knowledge of balm locations, as well as his wealth," said Nod. "To gain his help, she probably filled his head with a tantalizing lie, that they'd collect the fountain of youth and sell it to the highest bidder. But she's been planning a double cross. She stole my notes and letters, you see, and she's been privy to my thoughts about the balm."

"And you've been cryptic about those notes from the beginning," said Ellen. "You've told us you're worried about her mixing the balms. Why is that so bad?"

Nod gestured at the crater. "The balm—we've seen how explosive it is, eh? A little direct flame, and *bla-boom*! When Ringmaster Benedict told me other springs existed—and that they too were equally volatile—I thought the substance would be identical in each place. But something is different at each spring."

"Pet," said Ellen. "And its cousins. The *Nepenthes* plants too. All similar, yet slightly different. So?"

Nod leaped atop a fallen tree trunk with a mad look in his eyes. "An innocent detail to you, perhaps! But it is our first clue that *the balms may also be slightly different*."

"Okay, but again I say: So?" said Ellen.

"Ellen, you impertinent tadpole!" thundered Nod.

"If one balm can destroy a mountain, what might happen if it were combined with another compatible explosive? Drop a pebble in a pond and watch the ripples—if you drop another pebble in just the right way, the ripples redouble their strength. Might it not also be true of the balm? With each new ingredient, might it not grow more destructive still?"

"A superweapon," breathed Edgar.

"The likes of which we've never seen!" Nod cried. "A *balm bomb* that could crack continents! Throw entire countries into the sea! A person with such a weapon at her disposal could hold the world at bay . . . ask any price for mercy . . . demand complete obedience to her smallest whim!"

"Wow," said Ellen softly. "Stephanie is *so* much more horrible than I thought. And I already thought she was pretty horrible."

"Maybe she's destroying the springs as she collects her ingredients so no one can duplicate her work," said Edgar. "Does she have all she needs to make this balm bomb?"

"If she is collecting from every spring, she has just one more stop," said Nod.

"*Zimmizoka.*" Imogen whispered the name with traces of dread and awe. "The circus has never visited the place in my lifetime. Few Heimertzes have the courage to go back . . . the stories they tell . . . I mean, they're only rumors, but . . ."

"I have been," said Madame Dahlia. She smoothed her skirts and looked only at the ground as the others listened. "Fifteen long years ago, I have been with the circus. And we are not never speaking of it. The deserts of Zimmizoka, oh, they are cruel, but much worse is what lies beneath the sand. Buried deep in forgotten tombs the balm spring is flowing—and there the scent of death lies too. Ghostly and unhallowed. Unnatural."

"The scent of *death*?" said Edgar. "Are you kidding me?"

Madame Dahlia silenced Edgar with a swift gesture. She looked pained to say more, and when she did her voice was small. "The legends were old even in my youth. With each visit always came tragedy. Mysterious misfortune befell our clan always. The locusts . . . the flood . . . the fire that fell from the sky!"

"Good grief!" the twins exclaimed.

Pet cowered. Phoebe sobbed.

"So . . . who's up for Nod's Limbs?" asked Edgar.

"No, it's clear," said Nod. "Stephanie knows of the fifth spring. She is headed for Zimmizoka."

"Not necessarily," said Ellen. "She doesn't do well in the sun. It's that fair skin. It blisters up like you wouldn't believe—"

"Face it, children," said Nod, dropping a hand on each of the twins' shoulders. "We're desert-bound. Don't forget your sunscream."

"You mean sun*screen*," sighed Ellen.

"No, the sunscream is what you do after the sunscreen wears off," said Nod. "Let us restock the blimp with something other than ram bladders and prepare for a long journey."

Work began at once to restock the dirigible. They made several supply runs into Cougar Falls, which was putting itself back together. The town was mostly intact save for some debris and damaged roofs. A more pressing matter in the community was the absence of the now-demolished waterfall, and what that meant for the town name. (Seeing as how most of the forest animals had fled during the conflagration, the leading contender was "Cougar Run.")

As they worked, a bearded man in a dust-covered tuque came running into the campsite. He held out clumps of black hair in his hands to show Edgar.

"More than I've ever seen, Sally!" Gristly Jefferson exclaimed. "Whole tufts of it strewn all over the other side of the crater, like it was in a wrestling match—Oh, uh, hello, folks. You must be Edgar's sister and her blimp-loving buddies."

"This is Gristly," said Edgar. "He's devoted his life to the Squatch, Pet's cousin here."

"A kindred spirit!" said Nod. "Do you think the beast survived the blast?"

Gristly shrugged. "I can't say for sure. Finding this much hair is unusual—but what about the last couple of days *has* been usual?"

"We're about to go hunting for the person who did this," said Edgar. "You want to come along?"

Gristly sighed. "I definitely owe someone a wallop in the chops for what they've done to my forest. But . . . I've got to make sure my big-footed pal is all right. Thanks for the offer, though."

He and Edgar said their farewells in the fashion of truly manly outdoorsmen: they nodded at each other once and turned away.

In the meantime Nod huddled over some maps, making incessant calculations of prevailing winds, packing weight, and air resistance. At last he made an announcement to the team.

"Good news! With this dirigible we'll set foot in Zimmizoka three days from now," he said. "Of course, there's a catch: Only Dahlia and I can go."

"What?" the twins and the Midway Irregulars cried out as one.

"I'm very sorry," said Nod. "The rest of you may follow along by train. But for the blimp to make maximum time, it must carry minimum weight. Essential items only."

"You can't leave us behind after all this," Imogen said. She pulled an enormous box labeled "Marmot Jerky" from the pile of supplies. "I suppose *this* is essential?"

Nod gasped. "But it's jerky! Salty, smoky, fun to chew—and where else can I find it in this flavor? Oh, very well, if we lose the jerky we can take . . . well, look at that: Edgar and Ellen, you weigh precisely the same! Twins, you're with me."

The twins groaned but stopped short of refusing to go.

"We've got to see this to the end," Ellen told Edgar. "No matter how awful this desert is."

Imogen didn't take the news so bravely, however: She made a long and fiery protest about why the Irregulars should be allowed to ride along, but

Nod was quite adamant. His one concession was to eliminate a bag of maple butterscotch cups so Pet could join the blimp crew. Nod just barely calmed Imogen's fury by pointing out that only the Irregulars could be trusted to deliver Ormond someplace where he couldn't escape.

"I don't like it," said Imogen, throwing her ringmaster's hat on the ground. "All right, all right, we'll deal with Ormond. But by Barnum, we won't be far behind you."

Thus by day's end, nine would-be world rescuers (and one playful hairball) set forth to save the world from tyranny. When the blimp set sail above the pine-covered hills at last, there was no one left to wish them well—the irritated Midway Irregulars had slunk off without a word, carrying Ormond with them.

With heavy hearts Edgar and Ellen watched the world shrink away beneath the gondola and dreamed of catapults unbuilt, of trip wires untripped, and all manner of mischief and mayhem that was going unwrought in the world. They mumbled back and forth, planning imaginary pranks on the bustling citizens far, far below—plans that would all have to wait.

"Oh, try not to look so miserable, my striped friends," said Nod. "We're off to save the world! Who else can say *that*?"

Drops of cool rain pelted them from the soggy clouds above. They shivered as they realized that soon enough, these dreary drops would seem like a cherished memory when at last they passed under the unrelenting heat of the desert sun. But at least they were together again, and for the first time in many, many days, they sang as one:

From weathered woods to sun-scorched sweeps,
Across the sky our airship leaps,
To a place where mystery sleeps,
Buried in the desert deeps.
What waits for us in foreign lands?
What secrets sunken in the sands?
The race around the globe expands,
And still the lead our foe commands.
But, no matter what the weather,
Now we'll face this quest together.

THE END

Read where the

BOOK 1

Edgar & Ellen: Rare Beasts

Edgar and Ellen dream BIG when it comes to pranks. After they learn that exotic animals are worth tons of money, the twins devise a get-rich-quick scheme that sends Nod's Limbs into a frenzy!

BOOK 2

Edgar & Ellen: Tourist Trap

Mayor Knightleigh wants to turn little Nod's Limbs into a premiere vacation destination. But Edgar and Ellen have a plan to give the too-sweet townspeople all the attention they deserve!

BOOK 3

Edgar & Ellen: Under Town

Someone is causing a lot of trouble in town, but it isn't Edgar and Ellen! To catch this new mischievous miscreant, the twins must scour the sewers and uncover someone's dirty secret.

mischief begins . . .

BOOK 4

Edgar & Ellen: Pet's Revenge

Intruders invade the twins' house! But just when they need to stand together, one twin takes a sudden interest in . . . *niceness*? Now it's twin against twin, and somehow Pet is to blame.

BOOK 5

Edgar & Ellen: High Wire

A bizarre circus appears in the dead of night, and the twins try to join. They hope to skip town and escape the wrath of Heimertz. But nothing at a circus is ever as it seems . . .

BOOK 6

Edgar & Ellen: Nod's Limbs

Augustus Nod has launched a treasure hunt from beyond the grave! The twins must solve the riddles and discover Nod's lost golden limbs before the Knightleighs bury the past—and the twins with it!

With Augustus Nod back from the dead, the good citizens of Nod's Limbs don't merely tolerate pranking, they embrace it. They've even made Edgar and Ellen local heroes.

But all is not well in Nod's Limbs. Dirty tricks threaten the outcome of the town's mayoral election . . . and perhaps of slightly greater importance, the future of the planet rests in Edgar and Ellen's hands. The balm may have fallen into the wrong hands. Is it a new enemy? An old foe? Or the twins' archnemesis, Stephanie Knightleigh herself?

Book 1 of the Edgar & Ellen Nodyssey series

EDGAR AND ELLEN'S PURSUIT OF THEIR NEMESIS, Stephanie Knightleigh, leads them to Frøsthaven, an Arctic village whose cheerful citizens and strange customs remind them of home. What makes this place a sugary sweet duplicate of Nod's Limbs? The secret, alas, is upon the forbidden slopes of the Glöggenheim, where dwells something that doesn't take kindly to being disturbed.

BOOK 2 OF THE EDGAR & ELLEN NODYSSEY SERIES

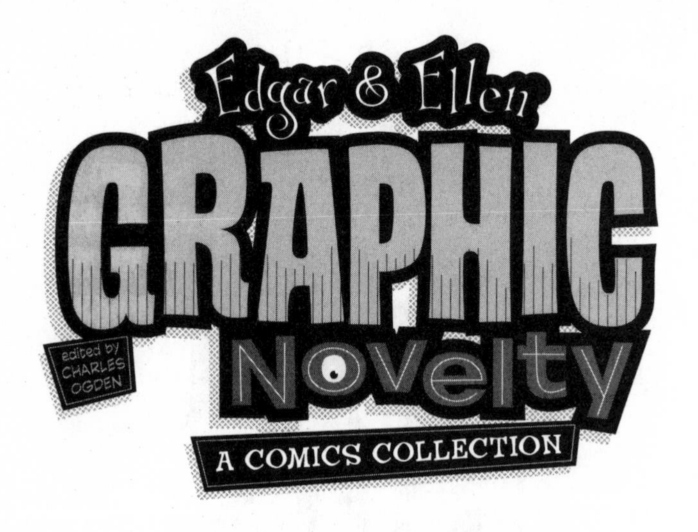

JOIN US, EDGAR AND ELLEN, AND EXPERIENCE FOR yourself the thrills, chills, and inescapable ills of our first adventures in comics! Now with real word balloons!

TREMBLE as we turn pirate and take over the Nod's Limbs Water Park!

WONDER as you witness a bizarro Nod's Limbs called . . . . Glob's Glums!

GASP as our manga doppelgängers show off their superior kung fu!

When you're in the comics, the possibilities are endless!

Coming Soon!

EDGARANDELLEN.COM

WHAT IS THIS PLACE? IT'S LIKE SOME OTHER UNIVERSE...
YOUR WORDS, BROTHER... THEY'RE OVER YOUR HEAD!
CRIPES!
GOOD GRIEF.
YOWZA!
ACK!!!
I'd sure like to borrow a nickel.
COME OUT WITH YOUR HANDS UP, POTATOFACE!
EGAD! NOT JUST ANOTHER UNIVERSE...ANOTHER MEDIUM! SEQUENTIAL ART!
...SEQUINED WHAT?
COMICS! WE'RE IN THE FUNNYBOOKS NOW, SISTER!
HA! THEY CAN'T MAKE A COMIC OUT OF US. ALL THAT CROSSHATCHING WOULD CRIPPLE RICK CARTON'S HAND!
Uh-oh. IT'S NOT JUST HIM. OGDEN'S IN ON IT TOO. LOOK!
That's right, Edgar! And a stable-full of brilliant illustrators and writers are joining in on all the fun. HO HO!
BUT WHY? WHY TURN US INTO SOMETHING AS CHEAP AND TAWDRY AS COMICS?
BECAUSE IN COMICS, ANYTHING IS POSSIBLE!
!!!
DON'T BE AFRAID. IT'S ONLY... COMICS!

Edgar & Ellen®

MISCHIEF MANUAL

AN EXPERT'S GUIDE TO PLANNING, PERPETRATING & PLAUSIBLY DENYING ALL PRANKS GREAT & SMALL (BUT MOSTLY GREAT)

Enjoy Edgar & Ellen? Add to the adventure at edgarandellen.com!

Enter the Wonderfully Wicked World of Edgar & Ellen! Become a reporter for the *Nod's Limbs Gazette* and use your byline to share the horrible truth! Write your own mischievous tales starring Edgar & Ellen! Watch the cartoon or play the diabolically great games!